Jake and the Kid

W. O. Mitchell

SEAL BOOKS
McClelland and Stewart-Bantam Limited
Toronto

JAKE AND THE KID

A Seal Book / published by arrangement with
Macmillan of Canada

PRINTING HISTORY
Macmillan of Canada edition published September 1961
8 printings through 1980
Seal edition / August 1982
2nd printing ...... September 1985

ISBN 0-7704-2102-4

PRINTED IN CANADA

U   11   10   9   8   7   6   5   4   3   2

Contents

1

You Gotta Teeter

IN THE loft above a pigeon flew some, slapping his wings to beat anything. One of the cats mewed. Stanchions clanked. Listening to the cows munching away on their green feed, I stood just inside the barn door with my throat all plugged up like when Jake plays "The Letter Edged In Black" on his mandolin, only worse.

She's real peaceful inside our barn at evening, but I wasn't feeling so peaceful waiting for my eyes to get used to the dark. Even with the milk humming "some-fun, some-fun", I was sad to my stomach. Nothing would ever be any fun any more. Mr. Churchill was gone, and he was gone for good.

I made Jake out. He was at Eglantine. Jake's our hired man.

"Jake," I said.

"Yeah."

"I looked all over like you said. I couldn't find him."
Talking isn't so easy when a person's throat keeps wobbling.

"He ain't gone fur." Jake only said that to make me feel good.

"I couldn't find him nowheres."

"Try the henhouse?"

"He wouldn't go there." Ever since that broody Buff Orpington took out after him Mr. Churchill hasn't been so fussy about henhouses.

"Better make sure."

"He – it's no use, Jake. He's gone for good! I know!"
Baldy stamped a hind foot a couple of times. Jake went on stripping Eglantine, and her milk saying "fun-fun" into the full pail: "If he wandered out onto Government Road," Jake said slow, "someone's sure to pick him up."

"But what if they keep him!"

"They won't." Jake picked up the chunk of cordwood he uses for a milk stool. He moved on to Bess, grabbed her tail, and held it along her flank. He laid his head against it. The milk drummed the bottom of the new pail. "They'd likely take him into Crocus – leave him fer somebuddy to claim. I'll make her to town tomorrow. If he ain't at the Maple Leaf, I kin try the pool hall – maybe MacTaggart's store."

"But what if he ain't there! What if he got run ov – "

"He ain't. He'll be there. No use gettin' het up. You git goin' on that there speech of yours."

"I'm not workin' on any speech."

"You gotta. Wanta make a mess of her? What'd yer dad over in England think if he looked in the *Crocus Breeze* yer ma sent him and it said, 'At the Rabbit Hill school concert last night, folks heard a shaganappy speech. It give everybuddy from Crocus to the correction line the heartburn. Nobuddy give a nickel fer the refugee kids!' "

"But, Jake, I – "

"Now, git!"

Outside was spring everywhere, with a warm chinook whispering along our poplar windbreak stirring our windmill tó creaking. Out on the prairie a million frogs in their sloughs set the soft night singing to beat anything. The whole darn bald-headed prairie was alive with spring, and I wished I was dead.

The nine-ten whooped a long holler to the night. Mr. Churchill was too little to know yet about coyotes and sloughs. Wandering alone out on an empty prairie he'd never find anything to eat. I'd never see him again. I wished I never had him at all.

Jake gave him to me. It takes Jake to bring a person the right thing; Jake's smart even if Miss Henchbaw doesn't think so. She may be a teacher, but you never catch her figuring out stuff the way Jake does; like how many grains of wheat she takes to reach from the straw stack in the south field as the crow flies, missing the bluff and the coulée, to our hog pens. All Miss Henchbaw knows came out of a book. Jake, he really knows.

Jake ought to; he's done everything there is. He's fought all kinds of wars; the one with the boors in it, the last war. It was Jake took care of Looie Riel; Jake he made Chief Poundmaker give in at Cut Knife crick. The history books don't speak so high of Jake, Miss Henchbaw says; according to her, they don't mention Jake at all. She keeps saying Looie Riel and Chief Poundmaker were way before Jake's time. She believes everything she reads.

It was her got all tangled up in the britching over me naming my pup after Mr. Churchill. It wasn't right, she said. Jake knew diffrent. Mr. Churchill would be tickled to death I named my fox-terrier after him, especially if it grew up and went after gophers the way Churchill goes after dick-taters.

Jake isn't so fussy about Hitler, and Mussolini, and Japs;

it's too bad those fellows in Crocus figure Jake's too old to
fight. They're not right. Jake may look old; his hair's grey
all right, but that hasn't spoilt his aim any. He's as good
as he ever was. I never saw Jake miss a gopher, or a crow,
or a skunk yet; they're a way smaller than dick-taters.

But I wasn't caring about any war now. Losing Mr.
Churchill made everything different. I didn't care what
kind of a refugee speech I made. I didn't care if it went
haywire. I didn't care if my dad read about it in the *Crocus
Breeze*. I was sure feeling a lot different about that refugee
speech than I did the day Miss Henchbaw told me I was
to give it.

That was the day I saw six gophers playing along the
road between our place and school. I saw crocuses too;
the whole prairie was patchy with them, and I kept right on
walking, thinking about giving a speech that was going to
help out refugee kids. The way I was, I was full up with
pop; the bubbles were lifting in me, not one at a time – all
at once.

At the corner of our pasture Queen's new colt with
knobby knees and a goofy tail romped like he was on stilts
gone crazy. I headed for the next field with black topsoil
smoking up from the centre where Jake was working. I
could hardly wait to tell Jake about my refugee speech.
Our best friend is a refugee. That's Violet; she's English,
and stays with Mrs. Tincher, that's her aunt, until this war
is over.

As I climbed under the barb wire, Jake at the far end
of the field was coming around on the harrow cart. I waited.

Violet was with me in the afternoon when I lost Mr.
Churchill. We played with him most of the time after four,
and I showed Violet the new calf that Jake bet was going
to be a heifer calf only it turned out to be a bull calf, and
Queen's colt, and the little pigs. Violet she thinks little
pigs' noses are a lot like milk bottle caps. She's not a farm

girl; she didn't know pigeons always have twins; she didn't even know what a baby chick's feet felt like to the palm of your hand. And that grey fuzz stuff on the bottoms of crocuses, she figures it's pants, to keep them warm because they come up so early. I guess being away from their folks makes a person a little funny. Violet hasn't anybody except Mr. and Mrs. Tincher, and they're only relatives.

But even if she is sort of funny, I and Jake like her. She's got sand, Jake says. I guess Cora Swengel figured the same way, after recess the first day Violet was at school – when Cora told Violet she talked funny. Cora had red slap marks on her face all through hygiene. Violet isn't afraid of anything. That was what made me think at first that, maybe being lonely and wanting a pup like Mr. Churchill, she'd taken him with her when she went home; but right away I knew she hadn't, and I felt ashamed of thinking it even. Violet isn't the kind that would take a person's pup.

"Whoo – uh!" That was Jake. He swung down off the harrow cart, and walked up to Baldy's head. He took out his jackknife, pushed up Baldy's collar, and began to scrape off the pad where it rubs against Baldy's sore shoulder. Then he turned to me, his eyes whiter than a Leghorn's egg, the rest of his face black with the south field on it. "How'd she go today?"

"All right," I said. "We're going to have a concert the end of the month."

"Are you now? That's real nice."

"There's gonna be speeches, and I'm gonna – Say, Jake, do you know how a person goes about makin' a speech?"

Jake stood there leaning against the fence post. All that dirt on his face showed off his teeth that came all the way from Chicago bright white. His mouth was red, real red. "We-ll," he said, "she's a long time since I made my last speech, but there's one thing I never forget."

"What, Jake?"

"You gotta teeter. If she's gonna be a good speech, why you gotta teeter. A feller might git by without fiddlin' with his watch fob, but not without teeterin'. Why, I remember the last time I seen Wilf makin' a speech. I kin see him like yesterday. Standin' spang in the middle of all them Senators and a whole slough of gold spittoons. The Senate had gold spittoons in them days. And Wilf Laurier he – "

"Sir Wilfrid Laurier!"

"Yep – that's him. There he stood, and there he spoke, and there he teetered. When he was through, there wasn't but one old Senator didn't vote the way Wilf wanted."

"Why didn't he vote too, Jake?"

"Never was known to vote fer nothin'. He was deaf."

"Say, I'll bet that's something Miss Henchbaw didn't know about – you bein' Sir Wilfrid Laurier's friend. When she hears about – "

"I wouldn't be any too hasty to tell her," Jake said quick. "You know how she is. Just like her to say it wasn't in the book. But history book er no history book, the good ones teeter. Why, I remember the last time I ever seen Wilf. Jake, he says to me, Jake, you know what? No, what? I says. Well, I'll tell you what, he says. If 'tweren't fer teeterin', I'd never of got the provinces to git together. Yessiree bob, them was his very words – if 'tweren't fer teeterin', there wouldn't have bin no Canada. And I wanta tell you here and now he could sure teeter beautiful. Useta use the water pitcher a lot when he spoke too. He – "

"Gee, Jake, that's great. You can help me."

"Help you?"

"Yeah. I gotta make the refugee one."

"Huh?"

"I'm gonna be the one makes a speech all about gittin' money to help the refugee kids."

"It's you that's gonna do it?"

"Yeah. Art MacTaggart's reciting, and Olga Wolochow's

doing the Highland Fling. Eddie Mike – "

"Well – why didn't you tell me right off you was makin' a speech? I didn't know she was that important. When did you say it was comin' off?"

"Two weeks Friday. It's gonna be in town – in the curling rink."

"Why, you ain't got but two weeks to learn to teeter in. You and me got work to do – after chores tonight."

Jake helping me had sounded good then but now I'd lost Mr. Churchill I didn't care at all. All I knew was I wanted my pup back, and I wanted him bad. I just had to look around our yard to miss him; my hand kept feeling lost for Mr. Churchill to pat.

Like he said, Jake went into town but he didn't find Mr. Churchill any of the places he looked; nobody'd seen him. Now he was gone everything was going haywire. Miss Henchbaw kept getting after me for not paying attention in class; I let a whole week go by without writing my dad that's in the s.s.r. where he's a sergeant in England. It'd sure not make him feel very good over there to hear about me losing Mr. Churchill.

Jake he kept after me about that refugee speech; only I didn't feel like practising it. The Saturday before I had to give it, Jake got me out in the yard by the blacksmith shop.

"Look," he said, "you gotta start stookin'. You ain't got but a week, and if you – "

"I'm not giving it, Jake. I can't. I'm gonna tell Miss – "

"Oh no you ain't. If them refugee kids could sort of quit eatin', and wearin' clothes – if they didn't have to have someone to look after 'em, you could turn quitter. If they could kinda feed 'em on somethin' that didn't cost money, why then she'd be all right fer you not to give that speech. Them kids gotta eat, you gotta orate, and by dang, you're gonna if she kills me!"

"But Jake – "

"Just because you was fussy about that there pup's no reason fer you to be goin' around with a mouth on you like you'd bin eatin' horse-radish through a wove wire fence. You think Wilf'd be mopin' around just because he lost his fox-terrier pup?"

"No, but he – "

"All right. Git a holt of yerself. We'll start from the beginnin'." He turned to where Baldy stood, looking sad with his head hung over the fence. "Baldy here, he's the chairman. I'll be the Ladies and Gents. You say, 'Ladies,' and teeter, then, 'Gents,' teeter agin; then turn and teeter to Baldy, and say, 'Mr. Chairman.' "

So I practised; I practised every day, all about it being a great honour like Jake said, and how I never seen such a fine bunch of people sitting down in front of me. And every time I got to feeling bad about Mr. Churchill, I'd think of those refugee kids depending on me to eat, and that helped a lot. It would have gone all right if it hadn't been for Mr. Brimacombe coming around the afternoon before the concert.

I always go down to our mail box for my mother, and when Mr. Brimacombe came by with the mail, I was waiting to see if he had a letter from my dad. He didn't, and just before he left he told about seeing a dead dog lying by the road a mile south.

I ran all the way back to the house, and told Jake. He wouldn't let me go with him. I wanted to, but he wouldn't let me go. Mother said no, too.

Jake wasn't gone long, and when he came back he said it wasn't Mr. Churchill, and for me to get in a last practice on that speech.

But it was Mr. Churchill. I knew. Mr. Churchill was lying dead on the side of a road, dead, and Jake wouldn't let me go see him. Jake was making me say a speech, and Mr. Churchill was dead.

I tried to go through it but I couldn't remember any of the words. Jake said that was just dandy, that meant I'd do good at the concert. He said Sir Wilfrid Laurier wasn't worth a hoot till he was on his feet in Parliament. Jake wasn't fooling me any.

In town, after supper, we dropped Mother off at the hall; I and Jake took the democrat round behind the Royal Hotel, and tied up. Then we started back for the concert.

Going down the street I kept feeling worse and worse.

"Jake," I said, "I don't feel so good."

"Where's it git you most?"

"I don't know. I – "

"Stumick all squoze up?"

"Yeah, and – "

"Knees got no insides to 'em?"

"That's the way it is. That how you used to feel when you made your speeches, Jake?"

"Useta? She's how I feel right here and now." Jake stopped. "Look," he said. "I'll see you later on."

"Why, where you goin', Jake?"

"Like I said, my stumick's sort of onsteady. Needs steadyin' real bad. Here's a dime. Go git yerself some pop at MacTaggart's. I'll meet you there."

But I didn't drink any pop. I couldn't. I went back of MacTaggart's to try out my speech on the hitching posts.

Mr. Churchill's nose was real black; there were tiny ripples over the roof of his mouth. You could feel them if you stuck your finger inside, only he didn't like that. He had freckles in there too; black ones.

I couldn't make any speech. I went in MacTaggart's.

Jake was already there. He must have steadied his stomach quite a lot. I could smell stomach steadier on him real strong.

"Let's go," he said.

The hall was fixed up nice; red and white and blue

strings of paper hung across the ceiling, and there were flags. She was full up with people sitting on the planks stretched across apple boxes for seats. You'd never know it was the curling rink only last winter.

I and Jake walked through the smell of shoe polish and chewing tobacco and shaving lotion and soap and all the concert smells; everybody turned their head and looked at me. I grabbed onto Jake's sleeve.

"Jake," I said low, "I'm gonna kick over the traces, Jake! I can't make any refugee speech. Not – "

"Oh yes you kin. If you fergit them words, you jist teeter. That's how – "

"But I – "

"We're all dependin' on you, Kid." Jake stopped. "Here's where I leave you. You're on your own now," and he was going sideways down the row to where Mother was sitting with Violet, and Mr. and Mrs. Tincher. Mr. Tincher's neck was hanging over his collar some, and I was standing there alone.

"Git!" Jake whispered. Everybody must have heard him.

I started walking past old man Gatenby that's got more boys in this war than anybody else in Crocus; I tripped over Mr. Biggs' leg that drives the C.P.R. dray out in the aisle. Right down the aisle I went toward the green curtains strung up front. An eye was peeping out between the curtains. I stepped inside.

It was Joe Biggs dressed in a sailor suit. Miss Henchbaw was sitting everybody down in a ring of seats there. I got one.

A few minutes later Mr. MacTaggart came back, and he asked Miss Henchbaw if we were ready, and she said yes. Ab Watson and Ike Ricky ran back the curtains, and everybody clapped, and Mr. MacTaggart stepped up to the front, and everybody quit clapping.

Mr. MacTaggart's voice sailed out, rising and falling like one of those gliders you fold out of scribbler paper in school. He didn't teeter any while he opened the concert.

Art MacTaggart was first; he recited "The Flag", and he did it good. Everybody clapped. They didn't know what it was like to have their pup dead.

After Art found his seat again, Eddie Mike played "When The Work's All Done This Fall" on his fiddle, and after him came Cora Swengel on the piano; she played fine after her third start.

In the marching to music, Jean Brimacombe was the war nurses; Archie White, the Army; Joe and Jim Bixton were Air Force and Navy, only Joe's uncle's cap, that's a sergeant in the R.C.A.F., slipped down over his ears and forehead so he couldn't see so good, and he marched into the war nurses in the hard part, and Miss Henchbaw went right on pounding out "Rule, Britannia!" so they got all bawled up. Miss Henchbaw looked around, and quit playing. Then everybody was clapping.

Mr. MacTaggart got up. He was saying something, but I didn't get it because Ike was leaning across me, whispering to Cora; they weren't scared; Cora was through her part, and Ike was just in the chorus.

Mr. MacTaggart was looking at me. He'd been telling them about my speech. I got up. I walked to the centre like Jake said. I stood. I looked at all those people. I wasn't thinking about any refugee kids. All I could think about was Mr. Churchill with a candy tongue, and him licking my nose and my face and my chin, and trying to get my ear to chew.

I turned to Mr. MacTaggart with his head shiny from the light above.

"Mr. – "

I looked down at the floor, and cleared my throat; it made an awful racket. I was breathing loud all over the hall. Mr. MacTaggart was still staring at me, and his head real smooth and glinty.

"Baldy – Mr. Chairman and Ladies and – and Jake. I

gotta make a speech. About refugee kids. It's all about refugee kids and – and I'm gonna do it too. I – you – it's a real honour, uh, to be able to speak to you – one and all. All of you."

There weren't any more of the words I and Jake figured out. I couldn't remember them. Mr. Churchill was lying dead on the side of a road, and I was standing up there with no speech to make. Nobody'd give a nickel for those refugee kids that needed it real bad.

"Look," I said, "I – I had a speech all figured out; I practised it, and Jake he helped me, only I can't give it. I'm awful sorry but – Mr. Churchill he died this afternoon. He got run over. He's dead now. I can't give any speech about refugees because he was my pup.

"You oughta seen him. He was red and he was white. He was a he. Jake got him for me. His ears sort of flopped but they were gonna stand up when he got older. He was a fox-terrier; he didn't act so bright sometimes, like when he'd growl pup growls at an old boot Jake left lie by the pump house. He'd of learned better. We were gonna catch gophers together; I was gonna buy war savings stamps with the money from all the gopher tails off of all the gophers Mr. Churchill caught for me. I – I guess I won't – now.

"You can't do anything about something that dies. You can't do anything about anything. That's why I've messed up this speech for the refugee kids. I'm sorry, I can't help it.

"You take around our place. You oughta hear Eglantine's calf bawl when she isn't near. Queen, she's gotta have her colt running by her side. It's the same with him. He nearly kilt himself on the barb wire fence when the gate swung shut on him and – and a chicken looks after its chicks.

"If you lost your kids could you make a speech in front of a bunch of people? You wouldn't remember about 'Mr. Chairman and Ladies and Gents and – and a real honour' and like that.

"Calves and colts and chicks and pups, they're the same as kids. Those people over in Belgium and France and England, the way they feel it isn't any different than with Queen or Eglantine or – or me without my pup. You wouldn't expect any of those refugee kids that's lost their mothers and fathers to be any good at makin' a speech, would you? Neither am I. I can't do it, and I'm sorry. I'm sorry I messed her all up. I'm sorry because those refugee kids need the money bad.

"Please – if any of you write my father, don't tell him about this. Mr. Cardwell, don't you say I give everybody from Crocus to the correction line the heartburn, when you write your paper this week. I – "

I quit. Down in front of me everybody had turned all spangly, and Jake and my mother and my dad and Violet would really be ashamed of me if I was to bawl up there under that bright light, with all those people looking up at me, and not saying a word; just looking up at me.

I hadn't even teetered.

"You done her, Wilf!" Jake was standing up out there with Mrs. Gatenby's hat all crumpled up in his hand. "What the hell you all waitin' fer!" he yelled. "Pass them plates fer the refugees."

That was when everything broke loose. I never heard a noise like that before in my life; it had the time that thrasher dropped his fork in McGoogan's thrashing machine skinned a mile.

Those refugee kids'll eat; $69.70 was collected. They thought it was $100.85 at first, and then they had to cut her down when Mr. Ricky realized he'd stuck in $31.15 he'd collected that afternoon from Mr. Metherall for back taxes. And they got to quit calling Mr. Tuck the tightest man in the district now; he gave ten dollars.

After it was all over, and I'd come down off the platform, Mother hugged me; Violet grabbed me and pulled me off to one side. Jake came too.

"You tell 'im," Violet said. I could see she'd been crying.

"About that pup," Jake said, "I told you it wasn't Mr. Churchill got run over. It wasn't. It was a collie – a black and white collie I'd never even saw before. You gotta believe me. Your pup's probably kicking around somewhere. Likely he's got a good home. He – you – "

"Go on," Violet said.

"Violet here, she give me an idea when she – "

" 'E's going to get you Mr. Churchill's brother that's just like 'im." And then she was crying again.

I looked at Jake; those fellows that take on soldiers in Crocus can tell best if a person's old; I guess they knew by Jake's eyes. He was sort of fumbling with that long rainbow thing he wears on his coat when he's dressed up; he got it from the last war he was in. He was looking down at Violet, and her bawling to beat anything. He said:

"You gotta figger her this way, Kid. That there pup he ain't dead; he's just a refugee kid." He put his hand on Violet's shoulder. "Some day he may come home. You – he – look, if you figger you could turn off the dang water works both of you. They wasn't only two in that there family of Mr. Churchill's – "

Violet looked up at him, her eyes wide, and her mouth part open. She'd quit all right except for a few hiccups she had left in her. "You mean to say you could get me one too?"

"Shore," Jake said. "They was six in the family."

"Wiv 'is tail not cut off?"

"Yep."

"And red and white?"

"If they ain't we kin paint 'em. Anything else you want?"

"Well – if it's all the sime to you" – she was squeezing Jake's hand hard now, the hiccups all gone – "could you mike it Mr. Churchill's sister?"

2

Women Is Humans

JAKE, our hired man, he didn't answer me right away, just looked at me with his mouth making like a round hole in the middle of his face; he was sort of squinting. He looked down at Mr. Churchill Two grinning up at us, his tongue spilled out the corner of his mouth. "Well," Jake said, "wimmen is funny all right."

What started Jake and me talking about women was my Aunt Margaret that had come to stay with us. It was her being so fussy about Bob Dyer, when there was a fellow like Jim Matthews around, that made me come out to the pig shed that evening when Jake was getting feed for the hogs. I'd said:

"Jake, there's something I'd like to know."

Jake went right on opening the feed sack with his jack-knife. I asked him again.

"There's something I'd like to know for sure."

"What is she?"

"About women."

"Oh." Jake straightened up. "Is that all?"

"They don't hafta shave – they smell fine, and they wear dresses, and they're prettier than men. Well, that doesn't mean they aren't humans, does it?"

So Jake said, "Well, wimmen is funny all right, but I guess you could stretch a point and say they was humans."

"Yeah, but you take how – "

"Wimmen is fussy about a lotta things that ain't worth a whoop. Like that there cow Eglantine. Ain't nobuddy but me kin milk her. That time I never had my blue smock on she sent me and two pails of milk clear acrosst the barn – rained two and a half inches of milk while I lay there. That's the trouble with a woman, they don't look past the outsides; hate to see anythin' that don't fit inta the pattern. Take that there cowlick of Jim Matthews's, and the way his good suit only fits him in spots. No woman kin stand that. She can't stand nothin' that ain't just so."

Jake always knows what he's talking about; Miss Henchbaw she sure gets the coal oil on her fire if you even get a decimal point out of place in arithmetic.

"But, Jake," I said, "the harness don't make the horse – "

"Fer wimmen it does. Clothes is real important to a woman – clothes and romance."

Jake was right again. My ma's always trying to get my hair into place; Sundays, just outside church, she takes her handkerchief pulled over her finger, and gives my nose and around my mouth a last rub with a little spit – mine.

"Is that what makes a person fussy about another person, Jake?"

"She sure is," Jake said.

So it didn't look so good for Jim Matthews; it didn't look any good at all, not when you got thinking of what my Aunt Margaret's like.

She's my Aunt from down East, and my mother's sister,

and a looker too. Her hair's blacker than new summer fallow after rain, and her eyes are like Ma's eyes are – brown brown. She's very small for a grown-up woman, but she's twenty all the same. Something else about her; the feel of her cheek. Take when she was leaning over me once, helping me with those per cent questions in arithmetic, and her cheek touched against mine. I never knew anything could be that soft – gentle like a pony's nose. Even if she was my Aunt I wished I wasn't a kid, and her growing older all the time I kept growing up.

This summer wasn't the first time she came to stay with us. That was why, when Jake and me and Baldy met the 8:10, there was a whole slew of Crocus boys hanging around the platform. Bob Dyer, that's a clerk in the bank, he was there; she ran with him some when she was visiting us the time before. While Jake and me stuck her bags in the democrat she talked with Bob, and when we were leaving he said he'd be seeing her Sunday.

In the democrat she asked how Mother was; she asked about Jim Matthews too.

Jim is very loose put together like he was joined with haywire. He's real tall, and the sun has yellowed his hair which is all the time flopping down over one eye. Jim has a kind of rough face so that he doesn't remind you of anyone else but him. Most of the time he doesn't say very much, and when he says it, she comes out very slow too. He has great big hands with knuckles, and lives on his own quarter section – alone, since his mother died two years ago.

But that isn't all there is to Jim. There's something important inside Jim he hasn't got a chance to say yet, and that's how Jim is. Me and Jake kind of hoped my Aunt Margaret would take to Jim the last time she was visiting; trouble was, she took to Bob Dyer too.

He's very different from Jim; next to Jake I guess he's the smartest man in Crocus district. His hair doesn't flop, or his cigarettes burn black at their ends; he wears a whole suit every day, and pulls up his pants every time he sits down. He has a this-year car, a blue one. "There's a young fella don't ever go light," Jake always says. Jake isn't too fussy about Bob Dyer, and that's because he has a way of running down the prairie whenever he gets to talking. Jake and me don't think he's a patch on Jim.

Jake and me think a lot alike. He isn't so fussy about Miss Henchbaw either. She figures because she teaches from a history book she knows it all, but she isn't so smart as Jake when it comes to wars. She never fought in any Boor war; she wasn't in the last one. Jake he'd have been over there at Dieppe with the rest of the South Saskatchewan if those fellows in Crocus didn't keep saying he was too old.

The Sunday after the Saturday my Aunt Margaret came, Bob Dyer wasn't the only fellow to call. About ten in the morning Joe Fister showed up, he wanted to borrow our wire stretcher, and after Jake got it for him he hung around talking. He was still talking when Rick Gatenby climbed through our barbwire fence. Rick had on his blue serge suit he helped his brother to get married in this spring, he was wondering if maybe Jake didn't have some Cobb's Bloat Cure for Cattle, Horses and Poultry handy.

While Jake was in the kitchen, looking, Ed James and Rusty Lammery showed up – they were both home on leave. Ed claimed he needed a scythe; Rusty was looking for some axle grease. Just before dinner Holgar Christensen came after a post maul, and then the boys were calling thick as grasshoppers. They came for: harness buckles, wagon bolts, bundle forks, nosebags, squares, bucksaws. Both Johnny Totcoal and Bill Johnson wanted our brace and bit. Jake he was wondering if there wasn't an epidemic of borrowing had hit the hired men of our district like that sleeping sickness hit the horses last fall. Every one of them stayed to sit on the front porch to talk with Margaret.

Jim Matthews showed up just after Bob Dyer. He didn't do so well with all those other fellows there, and Bob Dyer being such a good talker. It only took Bob one afternoon to get right back where he was with Aunt Margaret before she left last year. Jim didn't stand a chance with him pulling out her chair every time she got up, and pushing it under her whenever she looked like she was going to sit down. She seemed to like it, and that was why I asked Jake later in the evening about how women were different from men.

After that first Sunday it got even worse. Hardly any of the boys home on leave, or the ones that had stayed to run the farms, were left to hang around the bank corner, or Drew's Pool Hall in Crocus; they were all out seeing my Aunt Margaret. Noon Saturday they'd start dropping around; for supper there'd be three or four left over to eat; after supper they'd start coming again.

It was the second Saturday after Aunt Margaret came Jake got his first idea toward helping Jim out.

He'd just slid sidewise around Rusty Lammery's chair on the porch, stepped over Rick Gatenby's legs, and tripped on Ed James's where he was sitting on the step. Me, I was right behind, and as Jake headed for the cow barn, I heard him mumbling: "Hired men to burn!"

For about four steps he kept up that long canter of his, then he stopped short so quick he scairt Mr. Churchill Two into yiping in all directions, and startled a Wine Dot' and a Buff Orpington out of two years cackling. "Hired men to burn," he mumbled with a kind of faraway look in his eyes while he rubbed his chin. He turned and yelled from where he stood:

"Ed!" he yelled.

Ed turned his head from looking up at Aunt Margaret like she was a fat rain cloud building up on the horizon after three weeks June drought. "Yeah, Jake?"

"That there stock trough's real dry. Mind tyin' inta the

pump while I get these here cows milked?"

"Why, sure." Ed got off the step.

Jake started for the cow barns again, me with him – the woodpile's that way. Jake grabbed me.

"Just a minute," he said. He turned back again. "Rusty!"

"Yeah!"

"The kid's feelin' kinda peaked after all them measles he had. Would you mind lendin' a hand with a few birch chunks fer him?"

"But, Jake I ain't had no meas – "

"He's still got a few spots left where they don't show none," Jake yelled. "Doc said if he got het up they might bust out again." To me he said, "Let me handle this."

After milking he got Holgar to run the cream separator; it was Joe Fister and Rick Gatenby threw the feed down for the cattle; Hec Brand and Bill Johnson shooed the chickens in for the night. Bob Dyer kind of messed up that nice suit of his, helping Jim Matthews to fix the gas engine in the pump house.

Jake was all set for the boys when they showed up the next Saturday. Casual he started in talking about how hard it was for one man and a kid to get much done on a farm while the child's father was overseas fighting with the s.s.r. A little later he mentioned how his old Boor war wounds were kicking up something fearful so he couldn't do half the things around the place he'd like to do.

Later in the afternoon, when Aunt Margaret was helping Mother out in the kitchen, he told the boys about how disgraceful Aunt Margaret thought the fence along the lower oatfield was. It's been half down ever since my dad joined up and went to England. Fixing the fence and making Ma a lily pond were the two things he didn't get around to doing before he left. Jake could have built the lily pond, but he's funny about picking rocks. When it comes to rocks he's a lot like Mrs. Bingham in Crocus when she gets near cats. Jake doesn't sneeze like her, but he says even looking at a stoneboat gives him the heartburn.

It only took the boys one afternoon to put up nearly an eighth-mile of fence; Aunt Margaret sure had good fence builders calling on her; good rock pickers too. Jake organized a rock-picking bee in the south pasture the next week-end. That was when Ed James and Rusty Lammery dropped out. During the next two weeks the boys quit coming one by one. By the time the pasture was done, there was only Johnny Totcoal, Holgar Christensen, and Jim Matthews left working. Bob Dyer didn't get discouraged; he only called Sunday evenings.

It was the last Saturday of the rock picking I heard Johnny say to Holgar, "I'm sure glad we seen the last of them rocks. Even if the old coot figgers out more work, it's the last of them rocks."

He didn't know Jake.

Rick Gatenby and some of the other boys were back for more the next Saturday; word must have got round the pasture was clear. That was the afternoon Jake walked over to the pump, and paced off a few steps till he was under the poplar, then turned to the boys with a glint in his eyes. He said:

"Miss Margaret was just sayin' what a difference a lily pond could make to the looks of a place. Boys, we got the rocks; there's sea-ment in the blacksmith shop right now."

Even my dad couldn't have built a nicer lily pond – shaped just like a heart, spang between the stock trough and the hog pens. Jim Matthews was the only one left to finish her, and it was his idea made her a real lily pond. Jake said a person had to have goldfish for a lily pond, and I went to Jim and asked him if he knew where we could get a hold of some.

He started to say something, stopped like he'd been too soon for the words, then real slow he took another try at her. "Guess I know where you might – locate some."

"Where, Jim?"

"Special kind."

"Live?"

He nodded.

"Well, how long'll we hafta wait for them to come?"

He kind of tightened his mouth near the corners. "Got a piece of old window screen around?"

I told him yes.

"Chunka stick – broomstick, say?"

"Yep!"

"Right near here, in the river, we could get lots."

"Goldfish!"

"Not so gold, but they're goldfish all the same – prairie goldfish." I never knew that before. Me and Jim caught a whole lard pailful for the lily pond.

But even if Jake got all the boys except Bob Dyer out of the running, it didn't do much good. Evenings in the kitchen Bob Dyer did all the talking, running down the prairie; Jim just sat there with his shirt collar riding high, and his wrists showing red where his sleeves pulled up too far. His wrists are almost as big as my dad's.

He never said hardly anything except that time Aunt Margaret said, "You certainly know how to have sunsets out here. Last night was breath-taking."

"Nice all right," Jim answered her, his eyes stuck on the kitchen stove damper. "Sky caught fire like – "

"It takes more than sunsets to make up for the rest." The few times Jim ever got started, Bob Dyer cut him off.

Something else had to be done. I took it up with Jake.

"Like I told you," Jake said, "a woman's gotta have romance. Jim, he ain't got it."

"But, what's romance, Jake?"

"There's all kinds of it," Jake said. "Music romance – dang near got tied up with a Blackfoot girl once down near the border, just because I played 'Where Do The Flies Go

In The Winter Time' fer her on my mandolin. Powerful stuff, music romance."

"Maybe we could kind of hint to Jim about music – "

"Nope. What he needs now is pome romance."

"Pome romance?"

"Yep. A fella writes 'em pomes about how beautiful they are, and if they don't marry them quick they're gonna go hang themself in the barn on a halter strap."

"Maybe we oughta tell – "

"Nope; gonna handle her myself. Gotta make sure."

The first one was a dandy. Jake steamed a stamp off of one of the letters he'd got from the army telling him he was too old. He signed Jim's name at the bottom of our pome. I mailed it in our mail box out at the road the next morning. We sent three more that week; five the next.

All they seemed to do that I could see was to make Aunt Margaret look at Jim kind of funny when he came over. She seemed more interested than ever in listening to Bob Dyer, like when he was talking about buying the Davis house in town, and how it had good storm windows, and a new Pride of the Prairies kitchen range. She was real cool toward Jim.

And then Bob Dyer started going on about how terrible it was to live out on the bald-headed prairie. That was when Margaret looked over at Jim and said:

"I've heard that some people even become queer from the loneliness."

Jim cleared his throat. "It's not so bad as – "

"There have been many such cases in the annals of the West," Bob Dyer headed him off like always.

"Any recent ones around here?" Aunt Margaret said.

"Jist Old Man Froomby," Jake said. "Thought he was that there fella – what was his name?"

"Horatio," I said. "In the middle of the fourth grade reader."

"Yeah. Fer two hours he held the bridge over Bison river in Crocus – last Twenty-fourth."

"Did he?" Aunt Margaret said.

"Yep. Stood off the Elks' band, Crocus Durham Breeders, and the Presbyterian Ladies' Mission Auxiliary. Only had a empty MacMurray's Bluebell Brew bottle – forty ounces she was. The parade would still be there if it hadn't been fer the Crocus Boor War Veterans – "

"Did it take all those men to – "

"I'm the Boor War Veterans fer Crocus district," Jake said, "and Alex he had the strength of ten. Lucky thing I happened to have Jim Benny's two roan fire horses."

"But how did the horses help – ?"

"They was hitched up to the new chemical truck at the time. You know they must put some awful powerful kind of stuff in that there dope fer puttin' out fires. Old Man Froomby he turned a kind of – "

"That isn't just the kind of queerness I had in mind." Aunt Margaret got up. "I was wondering if there'd been any cases of younger men." She went out of the room.

She came back with a handful of papers. They were our pomes.

"I've been getting the strangest letters. At first I hardly knew what to think. Listen to this!" She read:

> "*I ain't so fussy about the flowers,*
> *Growed by the April showers.*
> *Crocuses and buttercups*
> *And vilets and buffalo beans*
> *And flax flowers too,*
> *They ain't a patch on you.*
> *It's you I'm fussy about,*
> *It's you I can't do without.*
> *I gotta have you like rain after ten years drout.*"

She looked up at Jim, and I'd sure hate to have her look at me like that. Her head was back kind of, and her eyes like I said were dark. They were dark all right – with being mad. Even her back, the way it was straight, looked mad.

"I can take a joke," she said, "if it happens to be in good taste. But this – these. I don't see how anyone could – " She quit; she was so mad she couldn't even talk.

"Why, they was real – I mean it sounded real fine to me," Jake said. "I don't know when I heard a nicer – "

"I suppose this is your Western humour. I suppose like your winters and your summers, it's extreme too."

"That poem didn't seem so bad to me," Jim said. "Did you ever see flax flowers winking like when a breeze – "

"No I haven't!"

"We can't all be poets." That was Bob Dyer.

"There ain't a thing wrong with them pomes!" Jake had got up off of the wood box.

"You neglected to mention pigweed in your list, Mr. Matthews!"

"But I – "

"Then there's stinkweed and – and – "

"Sow thistle," Bob Dyer stuck in.

I never saw Jake look the way he was looking then. I guess it was the first time he was ever in a spot where he couldn't say something to get himself out of it. And it looked like he was going to be in a worse one as soon as Jim told Aunt Margaret it wasn't him wrote the pomes.

"There's only one word to describe the person who wrote these," she was saying right at Jim.

"Well now, Miss Margaret, I wouldn't be too hasty," Jake said. "It ain't – he didn't – "

"Crude! You're a crude boor, Jim Matthews." She didn't mean the same kind as he fought in Africa, Jake told me later.

"I don't think you got the right – " Jim started.

"I'm sorry for you. I don't suppose it's your fault that you – "

"Just a minute," Jim cut in, and he had a look in his eyes I'd never seen there before. "I got no need for anyone to go around bein' sorry for me. You seem to figger I been sendin' you poems. All right, if that's the way you feel, go right ahead and think that; only I'm not simple enough to think that you're pretty as a crocus or a flax flower. You'd look sort of washed out beside a tiger lily to my way of thinkin'. Of course that may be the way I've spent my life, out here on the prairie."

He swung around. "And I've had about enough of listening to you bellyaching about the prairie, Dyer. You don't know prairie. You're like a lot of other folks that come to make a stake outa the prairie and get out as fast as you can. It's people like you give her a dry, cracked face with hot winds rollin' tumbleweed over. She was one hell of a lot different when my mother and father came out. She was rich then, and she was pretty. Why," he turned back to Aunt Margaret, "I thought I was fussy about you, but you ain't my first love. She's a blonde – straw blonde, my blonde."

I looked over at Jake; his mouth was open, his head on one side, watching. Margaret she was looking at Jim too.

"She's the kind of a woman makes a person think. You do a lot of wonderin' on prairie – on real prairie, not rollin' with bumps folks call foothills – "

"Burnt up in summer; frozen in winter," Dyer said.

"That's it – flatter than pea soup on a platter, with sky over top. I ain't never been away from it. I guess you don't find sky like you get over prairie anywhere else – "

"You sure don't," Jake said. "Why I remember when I – " He quit, and I saw why, Aunt Margaret had dug him in the side.

"Maybe being a dirt farmer is a miserable life, but it's a way to live. For a fellow like me that's fussy about dirt and

about sky, it's the only way. Maybe I haven't got a fine
house in town; I get a kick out of things that ain't quite so
important, like – well, like hearing what happens after a
meadow lark's heart swells up and busts, like clear well
water dropp – "

"A fine thing to give your wife."

"But that ain't all, Dyer – it ain't all at all. Look at prairie
mornings. When I was a kid I useta walk bare feet through
prairie grass cold with – "

"Are you going to take your wife walking barefooted – "

"Please, Bob!" That was Aunt Margaret. I never saw her
look at Jim like that before.

" – And sky. Prairie sky. There's something else my wife
will hafta hanker for. Once when I was a kid I dumped six
bags of bluing in my mother's wash water so I could get
the blue that belongs to prairie sky. Take the smell of wolf
willow growing silver along a crick – "

"A rather sickening – "

"The hell it is!" Jake bust out.

"Gentle honey, my mother called it. She loved the prairie
– she had to, the way she came out west with my father.
They didn't have a thing, not even a map for coming across
that sea of taffy-coloured prairie grass. Just a compass.
They come to where there were tiger lilies – millions of 'em.
She said that was where – and this's where."

Jim turned to Aunt Margaret. "Did you ever hear a lone
coyote on a winter night, making himself into a whole pack
by howling?"

"No, I – "

"Ever look in the throat of a tiger lily?"

"I've never had the – "

"They're freckled – their whole flaming throat is
freckled."

"They ought to call you the Prairie Poet." The way Bob
Dyer said that wasn't very nice.

"Yes," my Aunt Margaret said, "they certainly should."

The way she said it, she really meant it. She had a funny look on her face, just like the time my mother told me about how my dad kissed her in the smooth-on-barley field before they were married.

And after that night when Jim cut loose about the prairie I saw my Aunt Margaret look at him a lot of times the same way; more than ever, after Bob Dyer had quit calling. Somehow she didn't seem so fussy about listening to Bob Dyer talk after she'd really heard Jim Matthews go at it.

She seems to be pretty fussy about the prairie now too. She ought to be, because if she marries Jim like I heard her telling Mother, she'll be seeing a lot of prairie from now on.

One thing kept bothering me after that night. I asked Jake about it later. I'd been lying on my stomach, by the new lily pond, watching the breeze wrinkle over top, and the minnows darting below, and I'd rolled over onto my back to get a good look at the sky. There was Jake above me, looking down. And that was when I asked him. I asked him how much bluing she took to get prairie sky anyway.

"There ain't enough to do her," Jake said. "All the bluing on God's green earth won't do her."

He was looking sort of absent-minded off to where the new fence ran along the lower oatfield. "Bin a real fine summer fer vegetables," he said then. "Too bad yer ma don't have no root house."

He looked down at me again. "I was just wonderin', Kid. You ain't got no more aunts down east, have you?"

3

A Voice for Christmas

MA YELLED at me from the kitchen, but I ran out the back door; I wasn't waiting to put on my scarf, or coat, or toque, not till I'd told Jake. Just the way I was I ran – snow to my knees, the whole yard staring with it, deep, the soft kind you get when she's been an open winter saving it all up for a few weeks before Christmas.

The other side of the blacksmith shop I could see our barn kind of like a real red cake with thick white icing that wasn't put on so careful. It was Christmas snow, sparkly as anything; there were a million stars caught in the roof of our hen-house alone.

She wasn't so bright in the blacksmith shop where Jake was working over the forge. He was turning the handle on the old cream separator he had made into a blower, and bending over the coals the way he was made his face sort of blush up a soft orange, like a sunset.

Looking at Jake a person wouldn't guess right off how

much he's done for his country. He didn't do so bad in the
Boer war; and Jake was at Vimy Ridge. He even keeps
trying to get into this war. Last time was his tenth try, when
he darked his hair before he went into Crocus. The fellows
that take on the soldiers turned him down again. Jake says
he might have known they'd smell the shoe polish some.

He looked around when I came into the blacksmith shop.

"You oughta hear, Jake!"

"Hear what?" He reached down a pair of tongs from the
wall.

"About the radio. We gotta – "

"Ain't int'rested," Jake cut in on me. "You know dang
fine." He stood there with the tongs hanging from the hand;
he'd forgot all about the crowbar lying in the coals. "Why,
if they was to take ev'ry – "

"But, Jake, we got a letter from the – "

" – squawkin' radio in this here country, and lay 'em end
to end, and give me a holt of a axe – "

"But we got a letter from – "

"No wonder they ain't bin a decent crop in years – them
there radio waves ripplin' and skitterin' around. The rain
ain't had a chanct to fall. That's – "

"But this's all about the Christmas programme where – "

"Don't tell me about no programmes. Lookit what they
done to that poor fella last year – went right inta his house,
broadcast what everybuddy said round the table. Couldn't
let 'em eat their own Christmas dinner in peace."

"But, Jake, you don't – "

"Interference, they call it. It's interference, all right. Take
this here winter – a sorta long skinny fall, that's all she is.
Any snow? Not till last week. Blizzards? Nosiree bob; and
there ain't gonna be none neither, not with them radios – "

"Jake, this's – "

"Why, I never fergit the winter of o' six. So cold you
could see jack rabbits clear acrosst the prairie – froze. Froze

in the middle of the air, height about two foot off of the
ground where they leapt and got froze. One day I seen a
jack kinda squatted over a rose apple bush, about three feet
behind him a coyote with his feet drawed up right under
him ready to spring on the jack. Come spring the jack he
unfroze first; gotta head start on the coyote that way
and – "

"Jake, it's about my – "

"Same winter the Fister boys caught them a young
coyote; trained him to howl tenor so's he could carry the
harmony while – "

"Jake, it's about my dad!"

"Huh? What about yer dad?"

"We're gonna talk with him, Christmas Day, like – remember how they went clear acrosst Canada so's kids and
their folks could talk with their fathers that's overseas?"

"But you ain't – "

"I sure am, Jake. I got the letter right here saying about
what we gotta do."

Jake grabbed the letter right out of my hand. He looked
at her a minute. "We gotta be in that there stoodio four
o'clock Christmas?"

"Yep, Jake."

"And we're gonna hear yer dad?"

"Yep!"

"Talk with him?"

I said yes with my head.

"Chrissmuss!"

Up till we got that letter I'd figured on getting tube
skates and a hockey stick for Christmas. When I knew I
was going to talk with my dad in England, I didn't care if
I used bob skates till I was as old as Jake. And Ma – take
that night when I asked for another piece of bread and
butter and peanut butter; she just looked across the kitchen
table at me, her dark eyes starey and wide. I figured for a

minute the coal oil lamp was doing things to her mouth –
flickering like a yellow moth's wing, making her mouth like
that. Then her chin went, sort of, and she out the kitchen.

Jake he looked up from where he was hunched over his
saskatoon pie.

"I didn't do nothing," I said.

"Wimmen is kinda soft:"

"But, why did she hafta – ?"

"Wasn't nothin' you done; the peanut butter done it."

"Peanut butter?"

Kind of absent-minded Jake had his eye on the butter
dish. "Hayin' time or harvest she always brung lunch out
to me an' yer dad. Yer dad was always fussy about peanut
butter sanwiches."

A purple saskatoon berry out of his pie was jiggling in
the stubble at the corner of Jake's mouth. While he fumbled
with his knife, he stared down at the oilcloth. "Always had
to bring three or four extry fer yore dad." He pushed the
butter dish nearer him with his knife, next his pie plate.
"Wimmen always gotta blow the little things up twicet their
size – ain't the stuff in wimmen they is in men. Not like –
like in us, Kid." He'd finished buttering his pie; I never
knew Jake to eat butter on pie before; I never knew anyone to eat butter on saskatoon pie.

Next day after we got the letter telling about talking to
my dad, I could hardly wait to see Violet and the other
kids; Violet she's from England, and stays with Mrs.
Tincher till this war is over. I was dressing fast as I could
by the kitchen stove, and it cracking its knuckles to beat
anything. Jake was coming in and out while he did the
morning chores; Ma making pancakes. I never wanted to
get to school so much in all my life. Nobody in our district
was ever broadcasters before.

I was so excited I almost forgot to go out and feed Milk.
Milk she's what you call a squirt cat; all the time she sits

next to Jake when he's milking, and she waits for him to send her a squirt – so she's a squirt cat. She's grey, and death on gophers in summer, and was going to have some kittens. I'm fussy about Milk; my dad gave her to me just before he went to fight, and he said to take good care of her. Her going to have kittens would be just like getting a bunch of presents from my dad, and him way over in England – Christmas kittens.

After I'd fed Milk, I headed for school, Mr. Churchill Two ahead of me. It was his first snow, and he sure liked it – bouncy he went, the way Jake says he saw a jack go. I guess he figured it made him go faster. He'd stick his nose deep in the snow, and push her along, then lift his head and chew like anything, and shake his head, and come running back to me. He was fussy about the prairie in winter; anybody would be, with her all lard-white the way she was, stretching wide to where the sky started, soft grey the way it is in winter. You could hardly tell where the prairie quit; I never heard her so still – clean, cold, still.

Coming home from school I noticed it wasn't so still; she'd turned whispery with the wind that had started her smoking – thin snow smoke breathing off the drifts here and there across the prairie. Over the horizon the sky wasn't soft grey any more. Dark.

That was when I began to get worried for fear something might turn up to keep us from talking with my dad. What if it came a bad blizzard and we couldn't get into town with the roads all snowed up?

I asked Jake about it later on, after supper. "Don't you worry about no blizzards," Jake said. "They ain't gonna be no more blizzards like we useta have. Take o' six – there was the year fer blizzards. Old Man Froomby dang near went west that year. Stormin' so bad he strung a rope from his back shed to the barn so's he wouldn't lose hisself goin' from the shack to the barn to feed the stock. He folla'd the

rope all right – got hisself lost when he let go the rope and
stepped inside the barn."

"How come, Jake?"

"Wasn't no barn; wind took her right offa the door and
blowed her clear inta the next township. Old Man Froomby
froze so bad before they found him the doc had to lop off
his right leg."

"What if she blows up another like that, between now
and Christmas, Jake?"

"She won't."

"But what if – ?"

"Look," he said, "don't you worry none. Ye're gonna
talk with yer dad if me and you and yer ma gotta pile onto
Baldy's back to git into Crocus fer that there train. I tell
you she'll never be like she was in o' six."

I guess she was awful in o' six.

Jake was right, in a way; we had some real fine weather.
But about three days before Milk's Christmas kittens were
born was when Jake started being wrong.

This time the sky along the horizon didn't clear up; the
thermometer started going down, and she kept going down.
The wind, first she was just long soft sound you couldn't
tell exactly where from, and each day she was yelling a
little longer and a little louder. Three days before Christmas she was telling everybody across the prairies they
weren't going to live forever, crying like anything in the
weather stripping of our storm door, licking up the snow
and firing it in your face so hard you had to shut your eyes
when you were facing into it. Ma wouldn't let me go to
school the last day before Christmas holidays. Jake kept
right on saying she'd never be like she was in o' six.

Nights I listened to the wind howling around our eaves;
it didn't look to me like we were going to make her in to
take that train in Crocus, even if Jake said we would – not
if she got worse.

And she did; the thermometer in our back shed said fifty below just before I went to bed the night before Christmas Eve.

I lay there with my eyes right open in the dark. I couldn't sleep, thinking how we might not be able to get into town; I couldn't have slept anyway with the wind grabbing my bed and shaking it to beat anything, and the whole house creaking loud, and Jake in his room next to me. High over the blizzard I could hear Jake's snore, just the part where somebody grabs his throat, and he can't get his breath out.

It was Jake's snore started me thinking about Milk. Jake's snore always starts out sort of purry. I got to thinking about Milk and her kittens, just born. With that blizzard on, they could easy freeze to death up in our loft; it was full of cracks for the wind to get at them. My father told me to look after everything while he was away, help Jake with the stock, keep the trough full, give Jake a hand with unharnessing at night. Dad, he gave me Milk; she was stock too; she was special stock. I'd hate to have her kittens freeze while I lay in a warm bed. My dad never ever let stock shift for themselves.

I got up.

In the kitchen Mr. Churchill Two came out from behind the stove and jumped all over me while I got the coal scuttle and the lantern. He was too young for blizzards yet.

The wind slammed both me and the shed door against the back of the house. I couldn't get it shut again. The lantern flickered, nearly went out; I stuck it in the scuttle and headed for the barn.

Even with the wind at my back it was hard to get any breath; she was choking cold, kind of grabbing at the back of your throat the way an icicle sticks to a person's fingers. Between the house and the barn I only fell down once, but I got right up with snow down my neck, and up my sleeves. The lantern was still going.

I made her to the barn, got the peg turned in the door and opened her just enough to slip inside. I never thought I could be so fussy about a barn's inside. She was friendly warm, and sparkling something fierce with the frost growing everywhere; the walls and stalls and rafters winked and blinked and twinkled in the lantern light; some places on the roof she hung two inches thick, tufted – diamond grass. The knobs on Baldy's hames, the horsehair hanging on a nail by his stall, were crusted white with it; Eglantine and Baldy really had Christmas decorations.

Baldy didn't look round at me; Eglantine was down, she didn't pay any attention to me.

Up in the loft Milk raised her head, and stared green at me, without blinking. She didn't kick any while I put her kittens in the scuttle; they hardly moved at all. I didn't put Milk in till I got down from the loft; she'd follow me if I had her kittens.

The blizzard wind got me right by the throat, grabbed my nose, needled my eyes; going back to the house I was going to have to walk into her. It'd be real handy, I was thinking, if a person had their eyes and mouth in the back of their head. With the snow way past my knees I couldn't walk backward; all I could do was squeeze my eyes tight, put my head down, and try and get my breath with that wind doing its best to blind me and choke me.

Every once in a while I'd stop, turn around, and get my eyes opened. The lantern was out. I didn't care; all it could do was show me that stingy snow, alive with the wind lifting it and driving it against me, around me, down on me.

I wasn't getting worried any, not seeing the house yet; Jake always says she seems twice as far when you can't tell how close you're getting to where you're headed for. Only thing got me bothered some was the way my legs were getting heavier all the time; a person wouldn't think taking a walk between a house and a barn in a blizzard could be such hard work.

It wasn't till the second time I stumbled, and the snow threw me, that I got het up. Pushing into the snow with my mitt, I hit something hard, and long. I took another feel at her, then felt some more in the drift around. There were all kinds of them.

I stood still, the wind pushing hard on my back with both hands. I was by our wood pile. Our wood pile's on the other side of our house to what the barn is. I was feeling sort of scairt.

I was lost.

I lit out again, and I was thinking about how Old Man Froomby lost his leg in o' six. I was thinking how a person's feet and hands get cold even when they got shoe-packs and mitts on and are mostly warm from exercise like I was.

She was taking too long to get to the house; I wasn't getting any nearer I was sure. I stopped. I took my mitt off, felt in the coal scuttle to see how Milk and her kittens were. I stuck my mitt on quick so I wouldn't lose it.

I didn't know till later why I couldn't feel Milk and her kittens.

My legs were sinking right up to my knees in snow and I headed into her again. For all I knew now I was walking right through that black stinging blizzard, out onto the bald-headed prairie where Ma and Jake would find me in the morning – maybe not till next spring when the snow melted off.

It wasn't because I was tired I sat down. The reason I sat down, I wanted to sit down, so I sat down. I thought I'd have a little rest before I took another try at her, so I sat down for a little rest. My legs were sure glad I did it, and once I was sitting, I all of a sudden wasn't so cold any more; I'd got my second warmth.

They ought to sell snow instead of those hard mattresses; they ought to rig up some way to get the wind to sing people asleep. Lying in snow is just like in bed on a Saturday morning; just like after measles when you don't have to fight the wallpaper and the door knob and the quilt any more. Blizzards in these days wasn't so cold, Jake had said, and Jake was right.

In o' six she really was cold.

After a while I was hearing Jake's voice.

" – the year of the blue snow. Some folks claim you always git a blue shadow in snow when she's got a deep enough hole in her. That wasn't why she was blue in o' six; she was blue with cold in o' six. All the jacks acrosst the – "

"Just watch he doesn't get on those feet for a couple of days." That was Doctor Fotheringham from Crocus, and what was he doing in our house? From the foot of the bed I heard a couple of mews – big ones – then a lot of little mewings. "He'll be all right. They'll all be all right."

"Ma – Jake!"

My ma was beside me, and she was kissing me. Women are kind of soft.

After Ma had gone out with Doctor Fotheringham, Jake stayed at the foot of the bed, looking down at me.

"Well, you sure done her, didn't you?"

"My feet and hands, Jake, they – "

"Hurt like blue blazes."

"Yeah. I – they – I'm gonna – "

"Oh no you ain't. They just bin froze some. How's yer face?"

"Burny – oh Jake!"

"You ain't gonna lose nothin' – not like Old Man Froomby done. Doc thought he might take a little off of yer nose. I wouldn't let him."

"Thanks – Jake."

"I told 'm he oughta take off the head – round about the neck."

A person can always tell when Jake's kidding.

"What'd you hafta do her fer anyway?"

"I went out to get Milk and her kittens."

"You went out to git Milk and her kittens, and if it hadn't bin for Mr. Churchill Two you'd be stiffer'n a froze quarter of beef."

"Mr. Churchill?"

"Heard him whimperin' and yappin', and come down. Kitchen door was blowed open, and him runnin' to it and back again. We found you and them cats – 'bout as far as I could spit from the back shed door."

"Well, anyway it's turned out all right, Jake." He didn't answer me. "What's wrong, Jake?"

"Well, you – We ain't – " Jake quit.

"Jake, what is it?"

"I never did have no use fer them dang radios – "

"Jake!"

"Doc said you had to stay off of them feet. We – "

"Jake, I'm gonna talk to my dad!"

"Ain't nothin' we kin do about her, Kid. Doc said we could carry you downstairs fer Christmas dinner tomorra. That's all."

I didn't even turn my head away. Jake could see me all he liked. He went out.

I could see right out the bedroom window Christmas morning; Jake cleaned the frost off for me to look out. I could see our whole yard drifted with snow, the buildings bare, huddling around the edge; the windmill black against the sky. I could even see the rack, bare naked after the blizzard, wheels snow to the hubs. I wished I was dead.

I could hear them downstairs, getting dinner ready. For a while there were people going in and out the front door. I could hear them talking, but I wasn't interested; I didn't care. In the log cabin quilt Ma threw over me I counted the blue strips – faded blue; my dad's old work pants.

Mr. Churchill Two came into my room, jumped up on the bed, stood on my stomach with his head on one side, looking at me. He kissed at my nose, tried to push his face between my neck and the pillow. It didn't do any good.

I wasn't going to talk to my dad over in England.

"Merry Christmas!" Jake looked like he'd et a sunset. I said Merry Christmas too; I'd already said it to him four times.

"Git yer socks on. We're goin' down."

"I don't feel so much like – "

"Oh yes you do. You wanta hear yer dad, don't you?"

"Yeah, but – "

"All right, put yer arm over my shoulder."

Jake's strong; he lifted me like I was a light oat bundle; we started down the stairs.

Just before we got in the front room Jake stopped. "Now take her easy, Kid," he said.

There was a kitchen chair by the geraniums; there was a fellow I never saw before, sitting in it. He had earphones on him; he was sitting in front of our kitchen table; he was fiddling with the front of a big black box full of dials like on a radio. He was saying:

"Three – four – hello. Hungerdunger of Hungerdunger – Hungerdunger – Hungerdunger and MacCormack. One two three four – testing. One two three four – testing."

Jake told me afterward how he'd done it. He got on our phone the morning after I got lost in the blizzard; he phoned to the radio in the city, and he asked them why didn't they come to our place and broadcast like they did with that Christmas dinner programme last year. The fellow at the other end said no. Jake he argued, and the fellow said no again. That was when Central told Jake he couldn't use language like that through her switchboard.

Jake said he was sorry, and then he told the fellow how I'd gone out into the blizzard to get a cat my father gave me before he went overseas. The fellow said that was too bad, that it would make a real good story for over the air – he said something about humans – but he still didn't think they could do her.

Central told Jake to be careful again, and Jake said he would, and he asked the fellow why they couldn't send down a rig for broadcasting from our place, and the fellow said even if they wanted to they couldn't, on account of the roads being snowed up so they couldn't get through from town. Jake didn't get a chance to say anything right away with Mrs. Abercrombie cutting in to tell the radio fellow how her son-in-law took his wife in to have a baby in Crocus, and he made it all right with a bob-sleigh and team.

Old Man Gatenby, listening in too on the party line, he said sure they could get through; he did her to bring back the Christmas tree he forgot. Mrs. Pete Springer said Pete could easy meet the train and help them get their stuff out to our place. Jake said you could hardly think for all those people on our party line, making suggestions.

When he could get a word in edgewise, Jake said what if I mightn't pull through unless I heard my father's voice, and talked with him? And if they didn't send down the broadcasting rig my death would be on their head.

That was when Central chimed in and said they ought to be ashamed of themselves around that radio station if they didn't do something to save my life. The fellow said all right, you win – all of you.

There isn't anybody anywhere else in the world like Jake, or my dad, or my ma – or the folks on our party line.

We came right after the ones from Regina, and the announcer said all about me going out in the blizzard to get Milk and her kittens, and he said about Mr. Churchill Two, and I sat there with my stomach the size of my fist, only tighter, and my throat getting wobblier and wobblier, waiting to hear my father. Jake he was on the edge of his chair, leaning forward; he had a hold of the chair hard; I could see the veins standing out – blue earthworms crawling over the backs of his hands. I never saw Ma's eyes look the way they were looking then.

The announcer quit. For a minute all you could hear was

a sort of beating, wavy sound out of the radio.

"Hello – hello."

"Dad!"

"You all right, son?"

"I – I'm fine. You – hello Dad! It – Milk's fine too.

"Jake he – oh Dad!"

"You looking after your mother?"

I couldn't say anything; all I could do was listen while my ma talked to him, and he told her he'd got his parcels. And then he said:

"Jake there?"

Jake's mouth was part open; his eyes looked real tired – old tired – like they'd been looking against prairie sun too long.

"Jake."

Jake's mouth came shut. "Me? Why, shore, I – "

"You looking after those folks of mine?"

"Yore damn pertootin' I am!" The fellow with the earphones dug Jake in the side. "Huh? Oh – guess a fella ain't sposed to say, 'yer damn per – ' All right – all right."

"Understand you've had a rough winter."

"Hell no," Jake bust out without paying any attention to the radio fellow. "Little touch of wind odd times – some snow. Nothin' atall. She ain't bin a patch on o' six. She'll never be like she was in o' six agin."

4

Woman Trouble

SHE WAS dark in our back shed, and I could hear Jake's strop slap-slap-slopping to beat anything; then I heard the razor snicking against the palm of his hand. *Twinnnng* went the blade whilst he tried her with the corner of his thumbnail. He saw me then, and I could see him now my eyes were used to the dark. He said, "Hello, Kid," and I said hello, too, and I was wondering why was Jake shaving himself on a Friday night, only I didn't ask. She wouldn't be polite. Jake always tells me anyway.

I just stood there with the wind outside whining round the corner of our house, not soft and gentle like she's supposed to be in spring, mean; she was whistling with her teeth, clear across the prairie, so you wished you weren't a human being at all. I stood there whilst Jake went in and got him the lamp from the kitchen.

Jake came back out. I said. "Jake."

"Yeah?"

"Tuhmorra's Saturday."

"Uh-huh." He didn't sound like he was listening so hard to me.

"I was thinkin' of gittin' the washtub out."

He yanked a grey hair from the front of his head, nicked her with the razor. "Whut fer?"

He wasn't listening. Anybody knows about a washtub. You take lard pails, fill her up from the spring sloughs, pour the water down the hole where Mr. Churchill's run down a gopher. After three or four washtubs, or maybe five if he's the kind of a gopher that backs up the hole to plug her, the gopher's done for. Then you take his tail to the Municipal office in Crocus and they give you three cents for his tail; and when you got a quarter you take her to school, and Miss Henchbaw gives you a stamp to paste on Hitler's face. There's what a washtub on Saturday's for. Jake always comes drownding gophers with me.

He had his face all lathered up. I said:

"You figger you might have time tuh drownd out gophers tuhmorra, Jake?"

"Nope."

The storm door on the outside of the shed slammed hard with the wind. I never had Jake act like that before. If he couldn't make her catching gophers, he always told me why. He hadn't even told me the reason he was getting all shaved up. I watched him clear the side of his face, with the Old King Cutter curving down through the whiskers like a binder through ripe wheat; I could see the red, chicken-track veins all tangly over his skin where she's pulled kind of tight, like on a person's knuckle.

"Where you goin', Jake?"

He pulled out the pin feathers part of his neck – the foldy part – cleaned her off of one side and wiped the razor on his overalls seat. "Go git me a clean towel, will yuh, Kid?"

Up near the roller of the towel hanging on the wall there

was a good half-foot left. He didn't need any towel. He just didn't want to answer me.

Take the way he drank his tea at supper that night. Even my down-east Aunt Margaret noticed that. She's the one married Jim Matthews, and they had a baby last spring in our house. Whilst Jim's away getting to be a stoker in the Navy she's staying with us. She brought the baby with her. He's a boy.

She stared across the table at Jake holding his tea cup up with his little finger all hooked up like she had the rheumatism and he couldn't get her straightened out. About two inches under his chin he had the saucer like to catch the dribble. Aunt Margaret she looked at me; then she looked down at her plate quick.

"Have some more plums, son." That was Ma. I could tell she wasn't so fussy about me staring at Jake that way.

After supper Jake he out the door like a scairt jack, and he had the chores done by a quarter to seven. Then he headed for his room. Ten minutes later, in his brand new overalls, he came through the kitchen; the last I saw of him was the seat, with the red tag still on her, going out the door.

He shaved every night after that; you could see the basin with a pepper-ring of whisker bits round her rim out in the back shed any time you wanted. It wasn't for a week I found out where he was going – to Mrs. Clinkerby's that came to Crocus district with her son, Albert, to rent Jim Matthews' farm after he left for the Navy.

Mrs. Clinkerby was what you might call a square woman, and her arms were the fat kind with the tight skin on them that looks like what comes on sausages, only red. She was sure fussy about her son, Albert, that cracked his knuckles all the time and had an Adam's apple the size of a pullet hen's egg. She was all the time talking about what a good farmer he was. From what I saw of him he didn't look so

wonderful; he just looked very sad all the time, and I felt
kind of sorry for him without knowing why, till later on.

The next couple of weeks, with Jake going around with
his face all naked looking from so much shaving, I didn't
feel so good. Jake he sure acted different; he didn't have
any time to do anything with me; half the time he didn't
answer me; you couldn't say he was exactly mean – Jake,
he wouldn't hurt a fly. He went around acting like he wasn't
him and I wasn't me.

I sure felt a lot worse about her the night I went over to
Clinkerby's to get some baby bottles for Aunt Margaret.

Jake, he looked kind of startled to see me there, and he
said, "Why, hello, Kid," and Mrs. Clinkerby said to wait,
Dearie, whilst she got the bottles. She went out. I said:

"Jake."

"Yeah?"

"Who wuz she talkin' to?"

"Whadda yuh mean?"

"*Dearie!*"

"Dearie?"

"Me er you?" Seein' Jake sitting there on the wood box,
and remembering how he'd been acting ever since he
started in calling on Mrs. Clinkerby, I sort of spoke out of
turn. "I ain't so fussy about people going around calling
other people Dearie. She's enough to give a badger the
heartburn."

"Now jist a minnit, Kid. That ain't no way fer you tuh
talk. It's – she's enuff tuh – well – she ain't right."

Look who was talking! Whenever Jake isn't fussy about
something, it's enough to give a dog the heartburn, or an
owl, or a grasshopper, and the time Eglantine lifted him
and three pails of just-milked milk clear across the barn,
she was enough to give Hitler the heartburn.

"Well – I ain't Dearie, an' I . . ."

"Here you are, Dearie." She was back with the bottles.

Mrs. Clinkerby she asked me to set a while, and Jake he said she wasn't right to keep me from any chores I probably had to do, and I said I didn't have any, and I sat down. Mrs. Clinkerby she said we were sure having a windy spring, and Jake he said:

"Yep – she's jist like the thirties – once knew a fella name-a Candy – Jimmy Candy – section man fer the c.p.r., he wuz – wasn't fussy about rail roadin' atall – always hankerin' to git hisself a farm – when she come tuh blowin' so hard yuh had tuh lighta lamp dang near every day an' keep her burnin' till night when yuh could put her out, he dang near wore hisself out tryin' tuh figger a way tuh git hisself a quarter section out the top soil blowin' round."

"If he did," I said, "where could he put her down?"

Jake he stumbled around trying to figure that one out, then started in telling about when Mrs. Gatenby got a drop of water on her forehead someone spilt out of the upstairs of Maple Leaf café in Crocus. She fainted and Old Man Gatenby had to throw a bucket of dust into her face to bring her to.

Mrs. Clinkerby she laughed where you start in real low, and you end up real high. She smiled to me, too, only it came from a long ways aways, and her mouth had quit smiling before the smile got to me. I've seen other people use that kind of a smile before. They only use it on kids. She said for us to go in the parlour where the organ was, and maybe she'd sing for us.

She could sure sing; her voice was all full of soft hiccups. With that there organ going deep and slow like wading through water and her voice riding real high, and the song being "The Baggage Coach Behind the Train", it made a person feel like crying. Jake he was sitting way forward on the edge of his chair, and his chin was going gentle sidewise, and he had a faraway look in his eyes. Jake he's real musical on the mandolin. He can make a person want to cry too.

When she quit singing, Mrs. Clinkerby she swivelled round on the organ stool, and she said:

"Reminds me of my good man."

I asked did he die. I out with it before I knew; it wasn't very polite to ask a thing like that. She said no he didn't; he lit out the year of the 50-bushel crop, before they even stuck a fork in a bundle. Right there I commenced wondering why he didn't wait to cash in some grain cheques before he left, but I didn't say anything.

"Ef it hadn't bin fer my Albert," she said, "I don't know what woulda happened to his poor old mother."

"You ain't old atall, Mrs. Clinkerby," Jake said.

She hadn't been in any Boer War like Jake was, so I guessed she was a lot younger than him.

They had some trouble deciding what she should sing next. I said:

"How about 'That Grey-Haired Old Daddy Of Mine'?"

Jake he glared at me. The organ went *swoosh* with her bellows a couple of times, then she was groaning out "Little Joe, The Wrangler". In the middle I got up quiet and went out. Jake he didn't even notice I left.

There was me, and I was just a fly on a platter, the way she is on the prairie when you have a real moonlit night; wherever you go there's the black rim of the prairie round you, and some real far-off stars over top, and the wind in the grass like a million mad bees going all at once and everywhere. Just a fly walking across a black, flat plate.

The wind was so loud in my ears I couldn't hear my own thinking; I didn't want to, not all about Jake listening to Mrs. Clinkerby singing hiccuppy, and not being fussy about me any more, not wanting to drownd out gophers. I felt the way Baldy looks on a windy day when he stands with his head droopy and his hind quarters turned into the wind so his tail is laid right across his flank. Sad.

Jake he wasn't like Jake any more. Take the baby; he

wasn't even as fussy about the baby as he used to be. He never tickled him in the stomach with his chin so he'd laugh. With the baby he acted just the same as with me, like he wasn't fussy about him either.

She was about a week later, after I came home from school, I figured I better speak to Ma about it. I went in the kitchen, and I said:

"Ma."

"Yes, son?" She had a saucer and a bowl on the table.

"I was — what makes a person fussy about somebody?"

"Depends," she said, and cracked an egg against the edge of the saucer, then poured the yolk back and forth in the shell halves, caught the white in the saucer. "You mean like noodles?"

I watched her crack another egg. "No — not like noodles — like Jake he — well — like us about that there baby — like that."

"It's hard to say. It could be a lot of things."

I said, "But couldn't there — isn't there a sorta reason why — one important thing why a person goes around being fussy about another person? Isn't there one of those kind?"

She dumped the yellow into a second bowl she'd reached down. You don't use the yellows for Angel food. "Why?"

"Oh — I was just figgerin', an' so I wondered."

"So you wondered about Jake and Mrs. Clinkerby." She turned to me. "Tell me something."

"Yeah?"

"When the baby first came he was all red, and his eyes were bulgy, weren't they?"

"Yeah."

"Everybody came over to see him and said what a fine boy he was. They said he was handsome. Did you think he was?"

"Why — he wasn't no beauty."

"Were you fond of him then?"

"Oh – he – I guess so."

"Sure?"

"Well – mebbee . . ."

"The day that Tinchers came over with Violet – remember?"

Violet she's one of these refugee girls from England. She hangs around our place quite a bit. I said, "Yeah. Violet and me had a – a . . ."

"What about?"

"Nothin' much – how'd you know?"

"You were standing over the baby – you went outside then. I knew it didn't end there."

"Violet made me kinda mad. She said the way he looked gave her the pip. I just got mad for a minnit."

"Son, what makes you fond of the baby – enough to flare up when someone suggests he – he gives her the pip?"

"I don't know – it's . . ."

"He wasn't good-looking, was he?"

"No."

"He's not much good for anything, is he?"

"Why – sure he . . ."

"Can he stand up – like a colt – or a calf?"

"No."

"Can he feed himself?"

"No, he . . ."

"Has he got any hair – teeth? . . ."

"No, but – "

"People can't help being – fussy about a thing that needs them, son – whether it's a calf or a colt or a runt pig or a chick. If it needs you, you'll be fond of it."

"That's the way she is?"

"Yes," Ma said, "that's the way she is."

"And human babies is special."

"Human babies is special."

"But – but – Mrs. Clinkerby she ain't what you'd call helpless. She . . ."

"That's a little different. Yet it's the same – just backward. People are fond of someone they need."

"Jake he don't need her."

"Well – things are different now that the baby's here. Perhaps Jake feels just a little left out of things . . ."

"He . . ."

"Jake – just wants a little attention – somebody to make him a cup of tea – to talk with – do things for him. You know it's spring, son, and Jake has fewer springs to look forward to than you or I."

"But that's no reason why he – he don't care about the baby – or . . ."

"Oh, yes, he does. Don't you forget it. When a baby comes to a house people's noses sometimes get out of joint. Yours did a little at first. Right now Jake seems to have forgot the baby, but he hasn't – not really. He was fond of that baby before he ever met Mrs. Clinkerby – he will be again." She leaned over the cupboards my father made before he went over to fight. She straightened up. "You put someone's nose out of joint yourself."

"Whose?"

"Whose do you think?"

"Oh."

She started shaking the flour into the bowl with the yellows of the eggs.

"Did it take long to straighten out?"

"Did yours?"

I said, "Ma, I thought a person used the whites for Angel food."

That night, with the wind coming real fierce across the prairie, shaking the house, grabbing my bed, and shaking her right under me, I thought some more. Once in a while the wind would let up so I could hear the kitchen clock clickiting, or the house letting a couple of creaks out of her backbone.

A person was fussy about somebody that needed them

or somebody they needed – Jake he used to be fussy about
the baby – now he wasn't – he was fussy about Mrs. Clinkerby – maybe she could work backward – maybe the baby
could work her – no more Jake with his finger stuck out
like a hook – trade Mrs. Clinkerby for drownding out
gophers . . .

She's sure funny how a person can't catch themselves
going to sleep. I've tried. I never did her yet. I wait and
wait; then Ma's yelling the pancakes will burn.

All next day I thought her over, and the more I thought
the more she looked like that baby might switch Jake onto
the right track, from somebody he needed to somebody
that needed him. That evening the baby got his chance; Ma
and Aunt Margaret got invited over to Tinchers. I claimed
I had a stomach-ache, so Jake he couldn't hike her out to
Mrs. Clinkerby's as soon as he got shaved up. I got out of
an arithmetic exam that way once.

Ma she made me lie down, and Jake he muttered some
whilst she showed him where the milk stuff was, all fixed
up, and the bottles all boiled ready. She told him the diapers
were hung out on the line, and to bring them in after a
while and hang them in front of the stove so they'd be good
and dry when the baby needed them.

As soon as Ma and Aunt Margaret were gone I came out
to the kitchen. Jake he asked me was I feeling any better,
and I said a little bit and he looked at me kind of funny.
I said:

"He's sure cute, ain't he?"

Jake he went right on sitting there, and he wasn't in our
kitchen at all; he was sitting on Mrs. Clinkerby's wood box,
drinking tea, listening to "Bury Me Not On The Lone
Prairie"; he didn't care about any baby.

In Aunt Margaret's room the baby cried some, not much
– like he was taking a try at her, like he had nothing else
to do. He quit.

I never thought there'd be a time when Jake and me'd sit and not say anything.

The baby let go again; there was some temper behind her this time. He meant it.

Jake looked up.

"Fussin' a little," I said.

"How's yer stummick?"

"Fine," I said, and Jake looking kind of eager. "But she's fixin' tuh git a lot worse."

The baby was mad; sort of bubbly she started, and then, like a train whistling way off on the bald-headed prairie, she got louder and higher and madder and closer. It was sort of like when somebody drags their thumbnail across cement; it made a person's insides sort of hunch down.

"He's shore got good lungs," Jake said, and there was a good sign him talking about the baby. "Ef he hadn't he'd shore wore the hell outa them afore this."

The baby must of heard him. She was like he'd been crying on one lung, and he set out to show us what he could do on two. She went like V for Victory — ah-ah-ah-aaaaaaa-hhh! Jake he off his chair like a toad from a hot stove.

"Ma says don't go to him!" I shouted. "'Tain't fair to spoil him. Cryin's good fer his lungs!"

Jake settled back. He looked at me, and it seemed like the first time he really looked at me since he started in seeing Mrs. Clinkerby. "Ef I didn't know, I'd call enny man a liar who said all that was comin' out one paira lungs!" He was yelling; he had to so I could hear him over the baby. The baby had a calf at weaning time skinned a mile. Jake said something.

"What?"

"I said, 'They ain't no chance — git too much compression — crack a cylinder head!'"

"He ain't cried like that before!"

"Mebbe he's got somethin' wrong with him!"

Then I remembered; she was 8.30 by the kitchen clock. "He's sposed to be fed at eight!"

"Why didn't you say so?"

"You get him whilst I stick his bottle in the kettle to heat!" I yelled back.

The baby's eyes were all red with crying; he kept her up whilst Jake held him, waiting for his bottle. Jake he wasn't thinking about any Mrs. Clinkerby. Once I heard him muttering something about a woman's place, but I didn't get it good.

I gave him the bottle and he stuck it in the baby's mouth and the crying quit like throwing a bucket of water on a fire. She started up again.

"Whut's wrong now?"

I said, "Mebbe she's too hot!" I tried her on my arm like Aunt Margaret does; none came out. I'd forgot to take the skim off of the milk. All the time whilst I took the nipple off of the bottle, the baby kept her up; Jake he had what you might call a hunted look on his face. This time when I stuck the bottle in the baby's mouth, Jake sighed. He looked down at the baby and the baby looked right up at him; it had tight hold of his thumb.

"Shore is cute, ain't he," Jake said, "when he ain't squealin'."

She was beginning to look like Ma was right.

Jake set the empty bottle over on the kitchen table. Him and the baby looked at each other a minute.

"Jake," I said, "you gotta burp him now."

"Huh!"

"You gotta . . ."

Right there the baby's mouth opened; his eyes screwed up and his face went red; he started in hollering again.

"What'd you say?"

"You gotta burp him!"

"Whut's that?"

"Gas – he's got some gas in him the way he took down that there milk – pulled down air with it, and she hurts him – you gotta git her out!"

"How do yuh do that?"

"Stick him over your shoulder – slap him on the back!"

Jake he did, only he started in tapping him real light. He'd never knock any air out that way.

"Harder!" I yelled. "Ma sorta doubles up her fist!"

Jake nodded his head to show he heard.

"Kinda start down near the bottom – work up toward the . . ."

The baby burped real loud and loose. Jake he just stood there looking kind of startled, straight ahead. The baby grinned down at me, with his head turned sidewise.

"Jake!"

"Yeah?"

"You shoulda got you a cloth first."

"Whut fer – he's burped, ain't he? He ain't cryin', is he?"

"Yeah, but . . ."

"She's too late now." Jake leaned down to put the baby on the table. "Hey!"

"You got an awful lotta milk on that there shirt, not usin' a cloth like I said, Jake."

Before Jake got a new shirt half on, the baby started up again. Jake came in the kitchen. "Whut's eatin' him now?"

"I dunno. He's bin sleepin', so he ain't tired. He ain't got no gas and he ain't hungry. Mebbe he's . . ."

"That's her!" Jake said. "Whilst I unharness him you go gita dry diper!"

I looked all over Aunt Margaret's bedroom; I couldn't find any diaper. As I came out Jake said:

"Dry as the spring of '32! How do you git this here thing back on him?"

"Ma folds 'em three-cornered, but Aunt Margaret does her some other way where she folds both ends longwise, and back over each other so you git a piece jist wide enough to go round his stummick and pin on both sides, and she's real thick in the centre where . . ."

"Three-cornered!" Jake yelled. I watched him fold her. "This here's big enough to fit Baldy!"

"Fold her agin!"

"She's too dang small — guess you jist do her part ways!"

"That don't look like Ma does her!"

"I ain't nobody's Ma!" He stuck in the pins. "Last time you ever catch me around a baby!" The little muscles by the corners of his mouth were going, and that means he was mad. Ma was wrong about when somebody needed a person.

Jake picked the baby up, still yelling, headed for the bedroom. "Where's them dipers?"

I picked them up off the floor, where they slid from the baby after Jake picked him up. "They was a little loose, I guess, Jake!"

The baby still yelling, Jake put him back on the table. He didn't say anything, just took the pins out, spread the diaper, laid the baby on it.

"Ma sorts of puts her hand down in front to make sure she hasn't got 'em on too tight — to sorta choke him!"

Jake put in the other pin. He slid his hand down the front real careful, tested her for play. The baby quit crying. Jake's head came up.

"What's the matter, Jake?"

Real quiet, kind of hoarse from all that shouting, he said, "Go git me another diper."

"But they . . ."

"Didn't yer ma say they was some out on the line?"

"But they're all wet."

"Git somethin'! Anythin'!"

All I could find was two handkerchiefs, a dish cloth, some yellow curtains Ma'd made for the kitchen, and the little braided mat from the bedroom.

"See this here baby don't roll off of the table."

Jake came back from his room with a purple and gold thing of his. It said God Bless Our Home across the back of the baby after he got it on him.

But that didn't stop him from crying. Jake straightened up. He went to the phone, and he cranked her.

"You gittin' Ma and Aunt Margaret?" I asked him.

He didn't answer me; he said into the phone, "You better come over and give me a hand! We need her bad!"

He was phoning Mrs. Clinkerby. She hadn't turned out the way I thought. Ma was right. A person sure was fussy about somebody if they needed them. I'd only made her worse.

The baby didn't let up one minute. He'd hiccup some, and then he'd tear into her stronger than ever.

Mrs. Clinkerby she sure made it quick. Soon as she was in the door she turned to us, and she asked if the baby had his bottle, and I said yes, and Jake said he'd threw her all down his shirt. Mrs. Clinkerby said well no wonder he was crying; he needed more milk. As soon as he got it he shut up. He was asleep before he had half the bottle. We put him in his crib. Mrs. Clinkerby looked down at him.

"My, he's a lump, ain't he?"

I said, "Sure is, but he's all tallow – take a feel of them there legs."

She didn't. She said, "'Tain't enny too healthy fer a baby to be fat. My Albert he wasn't skinny, but he wasn't fat neither."

"I like the back of his knees," I said.

"Fat babies snore," she said. "Shows it's hard on 'em."

"And his heels – they're very pink."

"Mmh," she said.

"You take his stummick," I said, "when he's havin' his bath – she's all shiny with soap. He kicks like anything."

"The fat ones always seems kind of dopey longside the ones that ain't heavy."

"He don't act dopey," I said. I looked at Jake.

"An' usually they take a long time to walk. Has he got enny teeth yet?"

"He slobbers quite a bit," I said. "We figger he'll git 'em when they're ready." I looked at Jake again but he wasn't any help. "He'll git all he's got comin' to him."

"Little late talkin' too," she said. "Look at them chops and that there double chin. Now Albert was a real pretty baby – not – say – look at his head!"

"His head! What's wrong with her?" I said. She had me scairt at first.

"Flat – he ain't bin laid right when he sleeps. He shoulda bin changed from one side to the other. That's what I done with Albert. Albert's head is real round."

"I can't see . . ." I started.

"Better start lettin' him sleep on his stummick fer a while."

"You figger there's anythin' else wrong with our baby?" I said.

"Well – he oughta had teeth by this time. Albert had three by the time he was six months – two lower and one upp . . ."

"I don't care if your Albert had more teeth than a harrow!" I yelled, "er if his head was round as a snooker ball! This ain't Albert!"

"Well!" she said, and her mouth came together real tight. "It seems . . ."

"You ain't got no right to go around sayin' our baby's dopey, and flat-headed, and funny-looking – you . . ."

"Young man, when Albert was yer age he'd a got the flat of my hand across . . ."

"You never . . ."

"Now jist a minnit, Kid. That ain't no way to . . ."

I turned to Jake. "How kin you let her talk like that? You forgot all about when he gits a handful of yer hair and he tugs at her like a fish ona line! What about when he's asleep with his thumbs all folded up in his fists – and puttin' your nose in the crease at the back of his neck! What . . ."

"I know, Kid, I . . ."

"And how he smells after his bath – I . . ." She was coming up in my throat like water in a hole dug next a river. She was going to spill over. "Oh – Jake!"

"All right, Kid – she's gonna be . . ."

"I never seen such a spoilt . . ."

"Spoilt nothin'," Jake yelled at her, "jist smart – jist – hey, Kid, come back here!"

But I out the house. The wind caught me full in the face, drove the dust clear into the corners of my eyes; I could taste her gritty between my teeth. The whole sky was blown untidy with torn, black pieces of cloud, and the night was real fierce with breathing. The sound was coming from a million miles away, and she· was after every living thing. She was having your father over in England; she was Jake letting Mrs. Clinkerby talk about your baby like that, and not having any time to drownd out gophers; she was awful!

I don't know how long I stayed out there; when I figured Mrs. Clinkerby had left I headed for the house where the window still glowed like a square yellow coal in the dark.

Ma and Aunt Margaret weren't around yet; Mrs. Clinkerby was gone; Jake was on the wood box. His shoulders looked kind of droopy. I started to go past him.

"Kid."

I stopped.

"She's went."

I didn't say anything.

"She – she shore was mad – she – shore was mad."

"Was she?"

"Yep – went up like stumpin' powder."

"I guess – I – shouldn't have . . ."

"'Twasn't you set her off."

"Huh!"

"You wasn't the only one flew offa the handle. Think I wuz gonna set there and let a teetotal stranger run down our baby?"

"But . . ."

"No wonder he lit out."

"Who lit out?"

"Her old man. She wuz yappin' fer 10 minnits straight and she never went over a single word twicet." Jake he kind of shuddered. " 'Nough to give a coyote the heartburn." He looked straight at me. "How come we ain't bin out after gophers yet this spring?"

"Why – I already . . ."

"Tamorra – after I got that there seed drill fixed up – afore chores – might take a crack at her."

I was thinking something. I was thinking something about my ma, and I was wondering maybe she was as smart as Jake.

I'll tell when I get her figured out.

5

Old MacLachlin Had a Farm

AS SOON as we get into the yard, I wished we'd come sooner, right away after Mr. Brimacombe said about Old MacLachlin not having his crop in yet. It wouldn't be so good if Old Mac had gone and died without anybody knowing about it. I sure wished Jake and me had come sooner.

Old Mac he wasn't around the yard; there wasn't much of anything living there; no dog came out barking; no chickens were strutting around, just a scaldy-looking rooster pecking at the bare ground. From one of the crazy fence posts a meadow lark said she was spring a couple of times.

I commenced to think how a farm can get old just the way a human being does, just like Old Mac with his grey hair and his mustaches like a couple of grey oat bundles either side of his mouth. All Mac's buildings had got grey, real grey. She's sure awful what the prairie can do to a yard that won't fight back; choke her with weeds; pile her with dust; there isn't any fence can stand up to prairie long.

"Look at there!" That was Jake. He had hold of my shoulder real tight.

"What?" I said.

Jake pointed over to where the seed drill was; it hadn't any wheels on it; they were lying beside it on the ground. But Jake wasn't pointing at the drill; he was pointing at Mac's cow with her udder swelled up, pressing against the sides of her legs. She was pulling some straws out of some old bundles left in a rack from last fall.

"Come on, Kid," Jake said.

I was thinking, please let there not be anything happened to Old Mac, and him with Fergus that's in a prison camp since Dieppe. Jake and me, we're fussy about Mac. He's Scotch; he talks with more burrs than you can pick up in a whole day after gophers. Jake and me should have gone over to see him as soon as Mr. Brimacombe, that's our mail man, came by and said that Sam Botten was angling around to put Mac's crop in for him. Jake claims when Sam dies they'll have to keep an eye on the Golden Gate; he says Sam'll steal her off of the post and make another trip back for the hinges.

There wasn't anybody in Old Mac's kitchen; there wasn't much of anything except an old cook stove in the middle of the floor. Jake he hollered:

"Mac!"

There wasn't any answer. Jake yelled again.

I heard some springs creak in the next room, then:

"Aye?"

We went in.

Even under a log-cabin quilt Old Mac looked big; his both legs lay big down the bed; his hair all mussed up from lying there made his head look bigger than she really was. His eyes they were sort of mad-looking, real fierce under those clumpy-looking eyebrows like grey bunches of wolf willow. There was silver stubble growing bristly out of his face.

On the table beside the cot there was his pipe and a plate half full of old porridge. There was a picture of Fergus, too, with a real broad smile and kilts.

"Ennythin' the matter?" Jake asked.

Old Mac grunted.

"You all right?"

"Aye."

"Funny time a day fer a fella tuh be takin' him a lay-down."

Old Mac just kept right on staring up at us.

"Funny time a day fer . . ."

"I haird ye the furst time. Canna mon no ha'e a rest wi'oot the whole district comin' argy-bargyin' aroon!"

"Nope," Jake said. "Not if he ain't gittin' no crop in this late in thuh spring."

"Is that so? Do ye tell." Old Mac had started to sit up, only he lay back real quick like something grabbed him and she hurt.

Jake grabbed for the corner of the quilt. "Looks like you ain't . . ."

" 'Tis nothin' at a', an' I'll ask ye tae . . ."

Jake yanked back the quilt. I never saw anybody with a purple leg before; Old Mac's was, all the way from his knee to his ankle.

"Just a sma' bruise," he called it; he said he got it from the drill wheel falling on his leg. When Jake asked him some more questions, we found out the wheels had been taken off, at night. Jake he didn't say anything for a minute after Mac told him that. Then he said:

"Sam Botten bin around to see yuh?"

Mac said he had.

"Before er after them there drill wheels got took off?"

"Before," Mac said. "The day before."

Real slow Jake said, "Now ain't that funny. What'd Sam want?"

"He came fer tae poot in ma crop."

"Whut'd yuh tell him?"

"I'd prefair tae do it ma'sel'."

Jake he didn't say anything right away. I knew what he was thinking. He was thinking about a bay mare 15 years ago, the one Sam traded him. Sam said Jake'd be tickled to death to see her pull. When Jake got her home, he found out she couldn't pull taffy. Jake told Sam about it, and Sam just laughed. He said she was just the way he claimed; Jake'd be tickled to death to see her pull, and it was just too bad she couldn't.

Nobody ever got the best of Sam. He's one of the kind doesn't go to the trouble of owning any land; he's got two tractors and a couple of combines so he can seed seven or eight sections each year. He does her on shares, and he's always got crops spread clear over Crocus district; whenever anybody's hard up, Sam he's right there to put in a crop. The other fellow always gets the short end of the deal.

Sam he makes money other ways too. He buys scrap iron, and horsehair, and pelts, and beer bottles. He's always offering a person 10 or 15 cents below the going price for skunk or weasel pelts. He's sure fussy about a dollar.

Jake got up off the side of Mac's bed. In a real gentle voice he said, "I figger she's jist about time somebuddy nailed that there Sam Botten's hide to a fence post."

Jake he started in nailing that night. But right about here is where I better tell how the history got tangled up with what came after. Most of the time at Rabbit Hill I don't do so well with history, because I get most of it from Jake, and Miss Henchbaw, that thinks she knows it all, says Jake doesn't know his history right. Whenever I write down Looie Riel was a tall, hungry-looking fellow that wore gold cuff links, chewed Black Judas tobacco, and had a rabbit's foot fob to his watch, she gives me D.

But lately I been getting an H, and that's because of Old Mac's coulée, that some folks call Indian Writing Place because on the rocks at the south end she's all covered over with Indian writing. Most of it is pictures like what the grade ones draw, all mixed up with other stuff, like Imma Shoelack loves Steve Kiziw, and Joe Broomshawe, Broken Shell, 1932; but of course she wasn't, the Indians did that. Ever since we started taking up when the Indians roamed over the Crocus district, I been spending a lot of time around Mac's coulée. Whenever I find an arrow-head, I take her to school and get a good mark. Since I started this spring, I've found a war club, the red stone part of a peace pipe, two dozen arrow-heads, a bone-handled razor, and three dozen beer bottles.

After we moved on to buffaloes, my grades got even better. I found seven skulls half-buried at the foot of the cliff where the coulée cuts down real sharp. And even if there wasn't good grades in her, I guess I'd be fussy about Mac's coulée in spring. Here's how she is:

Still, still as water, with the sun coming kind of streaky through the wolf willow along her edges – what you might call stiff sunlight the way she's full of dust dancing all along her. And when you lie on your belly at the bottom of Mac's coulée, you're in a world; she's your own world, and there's nobody else's there, and you can do what you want with her. You can look close at the heads on the wild oats all real feathery; you can look at the crocuses and they're purple, not out-and-out purple, but not blue either. If you look real close they got real, small hairs like on a person's face close to a mirror. And there's tumbleweeds caught down there; they make you think about umbrellas that got their cloth ripped off of them – like bones, only not stary-white like a buffalo skull. Dead plants are better than anything animal that's dead.

The day Jake and me found Old Mac with his bad leg, I walked home a ways with Jake, until we came to the far end of Mac's back 40, where the coulée is. I left Jake, so I could take a look around for more Indian stuff and buffalo skulls. When I got home for supper, Jake he had told Ma all about Mac. After supper she phoned Mrs. Tincher so she could call a meeting of the Women's Aid and they could rig up a sort of a plan where each one took a day looking after Mac. Right after, Jake phoned Dr. Fotheringham to go take a look at Mac's leg.

The next day Jake spent the afternoon over at Mac's putting the seed drill back together. After school I went over to give him a hand.

The first day two things happened: Sam Botten came over to see Old Mac, and Jake told me about the buffalo jumping pound. I better tell about the buffalo jumping pound first; she's tied up with what happened to Sam later on. You'll see what I mean.

I just got back from school, and I said to Jake:

"Jake, I got H in school today."

"Whut!" Jake straightened up, and he had grease clear across his face. "Has she bin gittin' after you?"

"No, I mean I got a good mark again in history. Brought in a couple more buffalo skulls."

"Oh," Jake said, "that's nice. Whut the heck's skulls got to do with her?"

"We're takin' up about the Indians and the buffalo. Say, Jake, did you ever see a pound?"

"Dang right. Ain't I had tuh go git Queen and Baldy outa . . ."

"Not that kind. Like the Indians had, where they run buffaloes so's they could kill a lot and git meat fer pemmican."

"Oh. Why shore. A course I seen 'em."

"What're they like anyway?"

"Why they're – uh – she bin tellin' you fellas whut they wuz like?"

"All she said was they was a sorta place where they run buffalo, herded 'em, then killed 'em."

"Well, I tell yuh. I seen plenty of 'em, and there wuz one partic'lar kind I – uh – invented myself."

"Did yuh, Jake?"

"Yep." Jake was looking off toward the coulée. "Whut they call a buffalo jumping pound – run 'em over a cliff, like – well – see that there coulée?"

"Yeah."

"Why do yuh figger yuh found so many arras an' skulls round there?"

"Why . . ."

"She's a buffalo jumping pound, the one I'm tellin' you about, the one I figgered out fer Chief Weasel Tail of the South Blackfoot in the early days."

"You mean Mac's coulée!"

"Yep, Mac's coulée. I can remember her like yesterday. Weasel Tail he come to me an' he says, Jake, he says, we gotta have buffaloes. We need her fer meat, an' we need her fer tepees, an' we need her fer moccasins. We need her bad, real bad. There's bin a sorta flint drout around here an' we're all outa arras. The pemmican we was savin' up from last year, the kiyoots got at her. He hitched up his britch clout – he was a great big slashin' fella, wore nothin' but a britch clout – he hitched her up, an' he says, my braves ain't touched off but a couple a buffalo fer two months. What we gonna do, Jake? I dunno, Weasel Tail, I says; an' he says, Jake, they's a lotta buffalo hangin' around only we can't git at 'em. You gotta give us a hand, Jake. She's got me beat, I says to him; an' he hitches up his britch clout agin the way it was all the time slippin' down on account of his belly bein' so shrunk up not havin' enny buffalo to eat. Jake, he says, you gotta figger her out fer us. Ef we

don't git no meat fer our stummicks we might as well go
throw ourselfs over the side a that there coulée. Well, sir,
right there she come to me, she come to me how tuh git
them pore Indians some grub inta their stummicks. Weasel
Tail, I says to him, you go git you all your braves, build
yuh a fence anglin' tuh meet that there coulée where she's
steep, then go round up ever' buffalo fer a hundred miles
around — herd 'em with a hundred drags behind and two
hundred swings to the side, trail 'em right into that there
coulée, an' there's yer grub."

"Gee, Jake!"

"Buffalo!" Jake said. "You never seen so menny in yore
life. Thousands an' thousands of 'em, thicker'n grasshoppers, large an' small an' medium-sized. Cows with their
calves a-bellerin' after 'em, beardy ol' bulls roarin' so's you
couldn't har'ly hear yerself think. An' dust — they riz a dust
that made her just like night fer 50 miles around. They
come on the run, slaverin' at the jaws . . ."

"But if she was . . ."

"Stampedin' like they wuz, the shrink musta bin somethin' awful on all them buffalo — musta dropped a thousand
ton to the mile — made a fella shudder tuh . . ."

"With all that there dust how could you see 'em?"

"See 'em! There wuz a million red lights a-shinin' through
the dust, a million red lanterns where their eyes wuz, two
million bloodshot eyes that lit her up. An' the smell — she
wuz enough tuh give a badger the heartburn — like the
inside of a blacksmith shop a mile square with a million
blacksmiths shoein' a million horses — that wuz how she
smelled. They wuz runnin' on smokin' hoofs — red hot, they
wuz comin' so fast. An' then they hit that there cliff where
the fence angled in. They wuz water there in them days.
Soon as them buffalo commenced to go over, there come a
hissin' an' a roarin' an' a blowin' — cloud a steam came up
from them four million hoofs hittin' that there water —

scalded 15 braves and 15 ponies to death. The rest got caught in the blizzard."

"Blizzard!"

"Yep. Never seen nothin' like it. Steam hit the dust, turned her to mud, an' she started in to mud. She mudded 15 feet a mud in half an hour – the first mud blizzard I ever see – 50 Weasel Tail's braves got smothered to death a-sittin' on their ponies."

I looked at Jake a minute. "Jake," I said, "that's real hist'ry. That's – hist'ry!"

"A course," Jake said, "I wouldn't go tellin' that to – to folks that are fussy about hist'ry book hist'ry – the kind that like her sort a watered down. She might be a mite too rich fer Miss Henchbaw."

But there was where Jake was wrong.

Right about there I thought of something. "Jake," I said, "you claim there was a million of them there buffalo?"

"Yep."

"And they run 'em over the cliff?"

"Yep."

"Where's the bones?"

"Huh?"

"Where's all of them bones? Oughta be more'n a few skulls left outa million buffalo."

"Yeah. Ye're right there, Kid. Uh – why – the way she wuz – say that there water jug looks kinda dry. Mebbe yuh better – oh – now I – they shore wuz a lotta them bones, a whole mile along that there coulée, hundred feet deep, wide as the coulée. Then we had them real dust storms a coupla years after – covered 'em plumb over. Jist take a look at that there coulée – only 'bout fifty foot deep, ain't she?"

"Yeah."

"Useta be she wuz two hundred in Weasel Tail's time. Them bones filled her a hundred feet; dust covered her over about fifty. Now she's only fifty – see? What you might call a reg'lar buffalo mine down there, Kid."

"Jake," I said, "like I said, that there's history."

I headed for the house to fill the jug for Jake.

She was Mrs. Tincher's day, and she was peeling apples with flour right to her elbows. There was a saucer full of crocuses on the table.

From in Old Mac's room I heard him growling; there came a creak out of the cot spring. Mrs. Tincher she dropped the paring knife and she hit for the doorway. There came another squeal from the springs like when somebody lights on them real hard.

"That's the way, Mr. MacLachlin," Mrs. Tincher said, "you jist hike that there log-cabin quilt up under yer mustache so's you don't catch cold."

The kitchen door opened and I figured she was Jake, till Sam Botten pushed right through the kitchen and into the bedroom. Me right after.

He stood there looking at Old Mac and like always he was sort of chewing; he stood there real tall and skinny, turned kind of sidewise, and I could see the corners of his jawbones going, where the skin was pulled tight across them.

"Heard you wasn't feelin' so good, Mac."

Mrs. Tincher headed for the kitchen.

With his eyes ringed like knot-holes, Old Mac looked up.

I could see he had tight hold of the quilt; he has very old hands, bumpy like tree trunks are bumpy.

Sam said, "Figger we might make us some kinda deal, Mac."

"We canna."

"Land's mighty . . ."

"I'm pootin' her in masel'."

"You've only got . . ."

"Why don't yuh go seed yer brother's?" That was Jake, Mrs. Tincher went to fetch. Sam's brother he doesn't live here any more, not since he moved back to the States and left Sam to sell his land for him. Sam didn't even try; he wrote there weren't any buyers, then harvested a bumper crop off of his own brother's land three years in a row.

"Why – hello, Jake," Sam said. He was turned kind of nervous to the doorway. "Dropped in tuh see how Mac wuz doin'."

"Not so well. Doc says he's got some of that high-dro-foby in his leg."

"That so?"

"Yep. Kiyoot."

Sam's jaw quit working; he swallowed; his jaws started in to chewing.

"Kiyoots is bad this year," Jake said. "Aim tuh git me a pelt."

"How?"

"Usin' a little ammunishun outa Old Mac's granary."

"That so?" Sam turned toward the door. "Wouldn't be too shore ef I wuz you."

"On yore way out," Jake said, "don't git too near that there well."

"I ain't likely tuh slip."

"Can't take no chances. She's the only well Old Mac's got."

I guess Looie Riel was beat before he even started to wrassle Jake.

But the next day after school, I found out Sam Botten wasn't beat. I didn't see Jake till just before supper, when I went out to get the wood for Ma. I met Jake. He didn't look so good.

"What's wrong, Jake?"

He pushed past me into the house. I followed.

"Jake!"

He grabbed the basin, dippered some water out of the hot-water tank next the stove, then out to the washstand. I waited till he finished wiping his face.

"What's wrong, Jake?"

"Sam Botten wuzn't foolin'."

"What's he gone and . . ."

"Old Mac's granary – ain't got enough seed in her to fill a hen's crop."

"But . . ."

"Sam he knew there wuzn't none when he wuz over to Mac's yesterday."

"Do you think Sam . . ."

"Shore he did. That there granary's clear down by the bluff. A couple a trips with that there truck a his at night was all he needed. There's tire marks in the dirt right next."

"What can we do? Get the Mounties and . . ."

"Too late fer that," Jake said. "Be thrashin' time afore we kin git her back."

"Wut you gonna do, Jake?"

"I dunno," Jake said, "yet."

All through supper I could see Jake was figuring. And after supper whilst I was doing homework, Jake he sat there on the other side of the table. He didn't seem to be getting anywhere.

Me I was thinking she's awful the way things go; nothing ever goes right all at once. Up till I came home and Jake told me about what happened to Old Mac's seed grain, I'd figured she was a hundred per cent day. Take at school in history when Miss Henchbaw started asking us what we knew about the buffalo, I told all about the jumping pound just like Jake explained to me. Jake he said not to, but I figured if I told her like she came out of a book, Miss Henchbaw would think she was just dandy. She did.

I got another H, and Miss Henchbaw said we'd take a holiday the next day, and go visit Mac's coulée, and see where the Indians run the buffalo over. Of course I left out about her raining mud and like that.

And then I had to come home and find out about what

Sam did; I guess there's got to be some wild oats in every crop.

I heard a cranking sound and I looked up; Jake was on the phone. He phoned for two hours, nearly 30 calls. He didn't say much, just said Old Mac needed grain for seed. On an old letter he marked down the ones that had grain to spare. When he'd made the last call, he turned to me. The way he looked, Sam Botten was beat this time for sure.

"A hunderd fifty-five bushels. Johnny Lammery and Pete Springer, that didn't have none left, is donatin' their teams and wagons to gather her up."

Jake he's smart.

We didn't have school the next day; like she promised Miss Henchbaw took us all to Mac's coulée. That was where we run into Sam Botten again. He looked kind of startled when he saw all us there, and Miss Henchbaw she got to talking with him and she told him why we weren't in school, and she told him all about this being a buffalo jumping pound, and she explained how the dust had covered her over, and think of all the bones of that noble animal the buffalo that were lying there right under our feet, and what a cruel slaughter it had been. She said even if the Indians did need meat, they didn't have to go and run over a million at a time.

Sam he said he never heard about her before, and Miss Henchbaw said didn't he know this was an old Indian camping ground, and wasn't there all the writing on the stone, and hadn't I found seven buffalo skulls this spring. Then Sam he said come to think of her, he'd read where they did discover a bunch of bones in a couple of places that had been covered over, only she was in Alberta. Right there he stopped, and he left his mouth open.

Miss Henchbaw she asked him what was wrong, but he didn't answer her; he was out of there like a licked rooster. There was a funny way for him to act; I decided I better tell Jake when I got home.

Jake he wasn't listening to any talk about pounds that night. Old Mac had baulked at taking the grain folks had gathered up for him; Jake had argued with him, but Mac wasn't giving one inch. " 'Tain't no use," Jake said, "she's got me beat."

"But isn't there somethin' . . ."

"Nope. They ain't nothin' nobody kin do. He's bin lyin' there like a old he-bear with all them there wimmen fussin' around him. Says he ain't takin' no charity – ain't havin' his land seeded with neighbours' grain."

"But he can pay 'em back when . . ."

"I never seen nobody so stubborn in all my life – stubborn as a badger – a dang, old, stubborn Scotch badger."

She looked like Jake was beat. All through school I thought about her, and she looked like Jake was beat. Jake was right; Sam Botten was just like a coyote, tricky. Take the way he was all the time chewing, even when he didn't have a chew of tobacco, like he never had enough to eat; and the way he was all the time looking at a person over his shoulder. Right about there I looked up and saw Sam Botten, up in front, right in Rabbit Hill School. Miss Henchbaw she was showing him my buffalo skulls hung up along the top of the blackboard.

I got to remembering how he acted after Miss Henchbaw told him about the buffalo jumping pound; he sure was acting funny. I guessed I'd better tell Jake for sure when I got home.

And after I told him, she was Jake that was acting funny. He stared at me, and then he bust out laughing so hard I thought he was going to choke; he even cried some, he laughed so hard. And when he finished, he said, "Come on, Kid, you and me's goin' visitin'."

She was still light when we got to Mac's. We found Sam Botten there. He was trying to buy Old Mac's coulée; he just got done offering Old Mac $50 for her when we got there.

"Whut yuh want her fer?" Jake said from the doorway.

Sam he turned quick, then he turned back to Old Mac quick. He said:

"There's whut I'm offerin'. Yuh kin take her er leave her."

"Whut yuh want her fer?" Jake said.

"You ain't needed," Sam said. "My bizzness is with Mac."

"Whut good's that there coulée?"

"I said you wuzn't needed."

"I sorta figgered I wuz," Jake said.

"When I want you tuh stick yer nose in, I'll ask."

"He says it's for tae get the gravel," Old Mac said. "I canna figure it oot. There's na gravel in the coulée."

"Kinda white, bony gravel, Sam?" Jake said.

"Kinda felt sorry fer yuh, Mac," Sam said, "laid up like yuh bin. No crop in yet – got no seed – figgered a little money'd go a long ways tuh . . ."

"Yeah," Jake said, "I notice you shore bin helpin' a lot."

"You keep outa this!" She was just like Sam bared his teeth at Jake for a minute. "Whut yuh say, Mac?"

"Weeel, since I canna . . ."

"Wherever there's a dollar I shore do reely on Sam's judgment," Jake said. "Now, I gotta hunderd dollars in the bank, an' she's worth it jist tuh see whut he . . ."

"Two hunderd," Sam said quick.

Old Mac he looked up at Sam kind of dazed.

"Three hunderd," Jake yelled. Jake he didn't have any $300 in the bank.

"Four hunderd!"

Old Mac he looked real flabbergasted. "I – noo that ye're gettin' sae high – I . . ."

Jake he did a funny thing. He let his left eye drop down at Mac, and he sort of nodded his head so you could hardly see. Then he started in coughing to beat anything, and he headed out to the kitchen like he had to get a dipper of water. He pulled me along with him.

He went right on out the kitchen; he wasn't coughing any more.

"Jake," I said, "why's Old Mac's coulée . . ."

"Kid, when I done her, I never knew helpin' old Weasel Tail wuz gonna pay me back double – seein' them there Indians an' Sam Botten both with their stummick full."

"But what's she all . . ."

"Reg'lar buffalo mine!" It was Sam Botten, and he was waving a piece of paper in his hand. "Same as in Alberta where they run her jist like a mine – buffalo bones at $17 the ton!" He looked at Jake. "Yuh ain't changed a bit, Jake. Fifteen years ago she wuz that there bay. Now she's Old Mac's coulée. Useta be a jumpin' pound – Indians run over buffalo by the million. We gotta war on now – need explositives, an' they're a-makin' 'em outa bones. Bought me a $50,000 buffalo mine fer $400!"

After he'd gone, I turned to Jake. "Jake! What'd . . ."

"Reg'lar buffalo mine," Jake said.

"Old Mac coulda . . ."

"Too bad Sam didn't come tuh the district till '21."

"Old Mac coulda had all them bones . . ."

"Nope."

"Well – if they was all . . ."

"They wuz, Kid, only I fergot tuh tell yuh one thing. This ain't thuh only war we had, yuh know."

"What's that got tuh do with . . ."

"Sam oughta knowed they had tuh have them there explositives last war same as this one."

"Then there . . ."

"Plumb slipped my mind tuh tell him. She wuz mined out in '14 – plumb out."

"Then there ain't any . . ."

"Kid, see that there fence post?"

"Yeah?"

"I've nailed me a hide to that there post – kiyoot hide."

Jake spit.

6

Frankincents an' Meer

MISS HENCHBAW she got up, and she stood there with her hands folded together across her stomach; her mouth was sort of turned up at the corners, like when she's got something to tell us and it's good. Jake he claims she always looks like a hungry goshawk, only he isn't fussy about her, not with her all the time saying he didn't capture Looie Riel and Chief Poundmaker singlehanded.

Miss Henchbaw she looked down at us; her grey hair, that's piled up like one of those round loaves of bread, was under the writing on the board:

"The girl plays with the dog. It is fun to play."

She waited for Una to quit whispering to Violet, and the pencils to stop their dotting sounds, and Fat to finish grinding on the pencil sharpener. Fat he's always sharpening a pencil.

Steve Kiziw, that sits in front of me, he was leaning back lazy in his seat, twirling his ruler on the point of his pencil. Steve has two brothers in the Air Force. Me I got my dad

that's in the South Saskatchewans. Steve and me have our
trap line together; skunk and weasel been running good
since the last of October.

"Children!" Her voice all the time goes up at the end.

Steve's ruler clattered to the top of his desk.

"Just three weeks till Christmas." She smiled and you
could hear the Grade Ones and Twos sighing all over the
room. "Time we were getting to work on our Christmas
concert." The Grade Ones and Twos sort of all squealed
together. "Now I've – Steve, sit up in your seat!"

Steve he sat up.

"I've been thinking that we – instead of getting a play
already made for us, we'd do something new this year."
Everybody was looking up at her. Beside her you could see
the orange flames flickering to beat anything in the school
stove. "We're going to make up our own play this year.
And – yes, Una?"

Una took down her hand. " 'Bout the Babe in the man-
ger, Miss Henchbaw?"

Miss Henchbaw sort of pulled her mouth up together.
"Why, I think that – "

"Er – thuh Three Wise Men." That was Fat by the pencil
sharpener.

"Them sheepherders," piped up Ike. His dad raises a lot
of sheep. "Where they wuz watchin' their herda sheep an'
they saw thuh northern lights – "

"The Star of the East, Harry – were watching – Sit down,
Willis." She meant Fat. She turned to the board. On one
side she wrote "Babe-manger", on the other "Three Wise
Men". She turned around again. "We'll vote."

"Didn't put down no sheepherders," Ike muttered under
his breath.

It turned out 11 to 10 for the Three Wise Men. We got
10 girls in Rabbit Hill. Ike he didn't put up his hand for
either one.

Ike he got picked for one of the Wise Men along with Fat and Steve. Miss Henchbaw she made Steve in charge of all the stuff we needed for the concert: broomsticks for the camels' heads to go on, red tissue paper and a light bulb for the campfire, candles for all the Grade Ones for when they were all dressed up in green tissue paper to make a Christmas tree out of themselves.

I got to be the Wise Men's hired man, only Miss Henchbaw she suggested they better call me a camel driver.

We made up a pretty good play, all about where the Three Wise Men are figuring out what presents they're going to bring, and they end up where Fat brings gold and Steve some perfume called frankincents and Ike he was going to bring meer, whatever that is. Fat had the most to say.

After four Steve and me kicked our way through the schoolyard. She'd been snowing most the afternoon, so the yard was spread white and the prairie had lost her edge. You could only see a glowey place where the sun was supposed to be low down in the sky. By our forts we built in the corner of the yard where the buck brush had its black arms held out, Steve burped.

He can burp whenever he wants to by taking down the air first. When he burps he can talk at the same time. Once he said five words and only used up one burp. You ought to hear him pretend to sneeze too.

"You gotta pelt thuh next one," Steve said.

"I didn't say anything. In our trap line we'd got 11 weasel and three skunks; Steve meant she was my turn to skin the next skunk. I didn't say anything."

We walked down Government Road, with the snow sort of squealing under our feet.

"Wonder if we got a badger this time, Steve?"

"Dunno – Oughta be a good play."

"Yeah. I didn't want to be in it much."

Steve said he didn't either, but he didn't mean it any more than what I did.

"Guess we ain't gonna have Henchbaw teachin' us next year," Steve said.

I stopped right in the middle of Government Road.

"Huh?"

"They're gonna git Miss Ricky that's at Broomhead – Old Man Ricky he's gittin' her."

Mr. Ricky he's down the road from us and he's tight. The last three years he's been chairman of the school board. I never heard about Miss Henchbaw leaving Rabbit Hill. I said:

"I never heard about her leavin', Steve."

"I heard my dad talkin' to Ma – he says Old Man Ricky's after the $15 a month board he'll git outa Louella. If she comes here to teach she'll hafta stay with her dad."

"What'll Miss Henchbaw do?"

"I dunno," Steve said. "Git her another school."

"Wonder if Ricky's daughter's like he is."

"Can't be no worsen Miss Henchbaw."

"No," I said, "guess she can't."

But I wasn't so sure. Jake and me we're not very fussy about Mr. Ricky. Take the way we can't even get a softball for the school out of him, and the way he's all the time kicking about us using up the chalk. He claims Miss Henchbaw lets us waste it, throwing it around all over. I never threw any. Every time he gets a chance he hints about Miss Henchbaw not being so good a teacher; Jake he sort of agrees with Mr. Ricky on that; he claims her history's shaky.

When I told Ma what Steve said she blew up. "Why, that's a shame! Miss Henchbaw's been at Rabbit Hill 20 years!"

"Twenty years too long," Jake said.

"She's been a very good teacher," Ma said.

Jake he muttered something under his breath.

"I don't think the people around here want to see her go."

"Well, I knowa one that ain't enny too – "

"This is her home," Ma said. "She – why I've never heard of anything like that in my life!"

"Ricky he's thuh whole school board," Jake said. "Got his own hired man, Art, on. Old Man Gatenby he ain't much good, him bein' deef. Ricky he jist runs that there school board."

"That isn't democracy," Ma said.

"Miss Henchbaw she isn't so democratic, Ma. The way she – "

"That'll do, son!"

Sometimes Ma isn't so democratic either.

The next week I sort of forgot about Miss Henchbaw getting fired. She didn't act any different in school that I could see. Steve and me were pretty busy with our trap line: two weasels, no skunks, one of Tincher's chickens.

Friday I went back to the school to get my Health book I forgot, and I was almost to my seat before I noticed. Miss Henchbaw's head was resting bent forward on her desk, with her hands made into fists and them by her ears. I stopped. I didn't know what to do.

I scuffled some with my feet.

Her head came up. A hunk of her grey hair had come out and it was hanging down by her ear. Her face was streaky. Her eyes were just as red as the Santa Clauses sort of marching along the top of the side blackboard.

Old people look awful when they've been crying.

I got out of there without my Health book.

When I got home I looked for Jake.

"Jake."

"Yeah?"

"I – I'm not so fussy about – about the way Miss Henchbaw – "

"I ain't fussy about her either."

"No – I mean – about Mr. Ricky gettin' rid of her."

"No skin offa my knuckles."

"Jake – I got to thinkin' – everybody makes fun of old maids, don't they?"

"Uh-huh."

"It isn't funny, Jake."

"Whut ain't?"

"Bein' an old maid."

" 'Tain't likely – '"

"It must be awful lonely, Jake – she's lonely – "

"So's a goshawk."

"But he wants to be – she hasn't got anybody, Jake – she hasn't even got anybody in this war – she – once Ma told me she had a fella she – "

"Who? Her?"

"The last war – he was at Vimy."

Jake's mouth came open and it stayed there. Jake he was at Vimy Ridge too.

"She's always askin' about Dad or about Aunt Margaret's baby."

"Is she?" Jake he's fussy about our baby.

"Gettin' old and not having anybody give a whoop about you – Jake, that's worse than hail or rust – something you can't do anything about."

Jake he nodded his head slow. He isn't so young.

"An' if Ricky he – Jake – she was bawlin'!"

That night Jake went over to see Mr. Tincher. The next day they started the paper around for people to sign saying they didn't want Miss Henchbaw to leave. It stirred up a lot of talk, all about how Mr. Ricky he was getting his hired man to tend the school stove and not paying him any extra wages but charging for a janitor all the same. Everybody signed.

In school we went right on like there was nothing wrong.

We had our play all memorized. Ike he'd forgot all about the northern lights. Steve and Miss Henchbaw they had an argument and it was about chickens.

Steve he figured she'd be nice to have some chickens around the Wise Men's bonfire in our play. Miss Henchbaw she said no. Steve he kept bringing her up and Miss Henchbaw kept right on saying no.

It was about a week after we made up our Christmas play that Mr. Ricky came into the schoolyard. If he wasn't all the time coming around to snoop he wouldn't have got Steve's snowball in the back of his neck, the one with the special centre Steve meant for Ike.

Mr. Ricky he got Miss Henchbaw to line all us kids up and he started in giving us a talking to about running wilder than hooty owls, and how we needed somebody to really give us some discipline. Every few words he'd say, "Section so and so, paragraph so and so of thuh School Act." He said he didn't blame us so much as he blamed the teacher that would let us get out of hand the way we were, and Miss Henchbaw she was blushing real red.

Steve he sneezed the way he can do.

Mr. Ricky, standing there with his hat still on and the flaps down so he looks like a goshawk with blinkers on, he said:

"An' I wanta know who threw that there snowball?"

Steve he went, "AAAaaah – whooooo!"

"I'm agonna keep yuh all here till I find out which one a yuh."

"AAaaaaa – whuhiiich!"

Mr. Ricky looked sort of startled at Steve. He began to say something, but Steve looked like butter wouldn't melt in his mouth. "Ain't no use in tryin' tuh git outa her – I'll find out ef we gotta stay here all night."

"AAAaaaaaaah – huh-huh-hu-night."

"Say – " Mr. Ricky took a step toward Steve. "You ain't

tryin' tuh – " "Aaaaaaay – huh – ho – noooooo!" She was
a wet one.

Mr. Ricky leapt back and reached into his hip pocket for
a handkerchief. "That's him!" His voice sort of cracked.
"That's thuh boy that done it!" He reached out and lifted
Steve up by the collar of his jacket. Steve's face started in
working again. Mr. Ricky let him go quick. Steve's face
straightened right out again.

Mr. Ricky he said likely the teacher wouldn't do anything about making sure it wouldn't happen again.

Mr. Ricky was wrong. I saw Steve's hands afterward.

After that Mr. Ricky spread all over about how bad us
kids were, and he said seeing the teacher couldn't keep any
control over us he had no way of doing his duty as chairman of the school board except by getting somebody else
to take her place the next school year. He said he felt the
paper everybody signed didn't change things a bit; the
folks didn't know how bad things were in the school and it
was time something was done about it.

Ma blew up again.

She said, "Something has to be done, Jake!"

"Ain't nothin' a fella kin do," Jake said.

"But – can't – "

"Ed Tincher he said somethin' 'bout holdin' a ratepayers'
meetin' – tellin' thuh board how they – "

"Then why – "

"Ricky'd run her – soon as thuh notices wuz posted he'd
git her all figgered out how tuh throw a monkey wrench
intuh her – all thuh time talkin' about that there School
Act nobody knows about – fella feels like a fool ef he gits
up tuh argue with him – can't open yer mouth but whut
she's wrong by section so an' so, paragraft such an' such."

"Why doesn't – can't somebody get a School Act and – "

"Why – I 'spose – "

"Does Mr. Ricky have to know about the meeting ahead
of time?"

"There's somethin' about yuh gotta have her up three places – I remember when – how kin yuh hold a meetin' ef folks don't know about her – an' ef they know, Ricky he'll know too. He – say! Kid! When's that there Christmas concert?"

"Week from Thursday, Jake."

"That's whut we kin do – folks'll all be tuhgether – hold our meetin' right after thuh concert – good time too right after a entertainment she got up – kinda soften folks up toward her."

All that week the weasels were running good. The night before the concert Steve and me took a badger out; his hair was real long and thick.

It was the night of the Christmas concert we got the skunk.

Steve he came over to our place for supper, and he helped me with my chores. He brought over his sheet for being a Wise Man all wrapped up in paper. Ma and Jake went over to Tinchers early so they could go to the concert with them. Steve helped me hitch up Baldy to the bobsleigh when she was about time to go. He threw his parcel into the back of the box. I went back to the house to get my Little Daisy .22; our trap line lies right on the way to the new Community Hall and we figured we might find something in her to shoot.

When I came back outside, Steve he had a gunny sack in his hand and he was tying the neck up and there were some squawks coming out of it.

"What you doin', Steve?"

"Jist borra'd a couple of your chickens for that there play."

"But – "

"Ain't nothin gonna happen – "

"Miss Henchbaw she said you couldn't."

"It'll make it a lot realer to have some chickens up on the stage."

"But what'll Ma – "

"We'll bring 'em right back after the concert. They'll be all right."

I didn't argue any more. How'd I know he'd caught the barred Rock and the Wyandotte? They bust loose every time they catch sight of each other. They're roosters.

When we got to the fourth trap there was a skunk in her. Steve shot it and he took it out. He threw it into the box of the sleigh. We went on to the hall, and the smell of skunk came right along with us.

Because he had to fix up the light bulb with red tissue paper and sticks for the Wise Men's bonfire, Steve went in the hall ahead of me. He took the sack with the chickens, said he was keeping them in the kitchen till it was time to use them. He told me to bring his other parcel.

I tied Baldy up to the fence then went to get Steve's Wise Man sheet.

The skunk was lying right on top of it.

The smell of skunk followed me to the hall real strong.

For a good 15 minutes before our play came on the folks out front could smell Steve's sheet, not so strong at first, Jake told me after, but when the curtain came apart she just leapt out at the audience. I know when I came onto the stage I could see the folks looking around sort of side-wise at each other, like they were wondering whether the skunk was somewhere in the hall or just outside.

Two of the Wise Men knew – Ike and Fat; when they came out on their camels there was a lot of distance between Steve and the other Wise Men. Even the two roosters Steve had turned loose just stood there on the stage, looking dazed. When I came up to take the camels away the smell sort of caught at my breath.

The way he was supposed to Steve sat up close to the bonfire; on the other side Fat and Ike were just as far away as they could get without looking as though something was wrong.

"What are we going to give, O Wise Men?" Ike's voice came out sort of muffled. He was holding his sheet up over his nose.

"We must bring the best presents that can be brung." Miss Henchbaw had told him not to say "brung".

"And what are you – goin' – to – what – uh." Ike choked.

Steve got up and started around the fire the way he was supposed to. "Thuh bee-you-teeous perfume of thuh East. Frankincents."

"I-will-bring-the-gifta-meer." Fat ripped it out; he was way ahead of himself, but it was the speech he was to make before he went off. He left.

"Me, I better throw down a bundle to them camels." That was real smart of Ike; it wasn't what was written in the play at all, but with Steve coming for him Ike had to think quick. He turned and ran. The light cord for the bonfire caught his foot; he took off and lit flat on his face.

The barred Rock rooster let out a crow and leaped at the Wyandotte, his feathers up around his neck. Then they were going at it, just like a couple of balls you throw up in the air and catch and throw up again.

Smell or no smell I rushed out on to the stage to help Steve get those roosters. He'd got one, was holding it squawking under his arm whilst he tried to get the other. Just as we got the Wyandotte chased off into Fat's arms, the barred Rock got away again, and we had to go through her all over again.

We'd sure messed her up for Miss Henchbaw getting back again as teacher in Rabbit Hill. I told Steve that whilst we were out getting rid of his sheet and helping to open all the doors to air out the hall. It didn't seem to bother Steve; he had his mind on the Christmas candy and pop they were going to hand out.

When we came back in the front of the hall Jake and Mr.

Tincher were up on the stage. Mr. Ricky was standing out in the audience.

" 'Tain't legal!" he was yelling. "Can't hold her unless yuh got yer three notices posted!"

"We posted 'em!" Jake yelled back at him.

"Where? I ain't see 'em. Where was they posted?"

"Backa our cow barn," Jake said. "One on Totcoal's windmill – 'nother on Ed's granary in his East forty."

"But that ain't – I didn't – "

"We're here tuhnight," Jake said, "tuh make sure thuh folks in this district get thuh teacher they want teachin' their kids. So we have – "

"Section fifty-three – paragraph five says – "

"We have met tuh direct our school board tuh – "

" – only ratepayers kin – "

"Will Mr. Ricky set down an' shet up!" That was Bent Matthews.

"No, he won't," said Mr. Ricky. "I've set here tuhnight an' seen thuh most disgraceful display I ever – "

"Fine concert – what I saw," said Mr. Tincher.

"Them roosters!" shouted Old Man Gatenby. "Most comical thing I ever seen!"

"Ain't bin so much excitement sence thuh Fenian raids," yelled Phadrig Connor.

Then they were all yelling what a good concert it had been, and they meant it. When they had quieted down Jake said:

"We're gonna take vote – "

"Section fifty-three – paragraph five – "

"Johnny – Bent!" Jake called out. Mr. Totcoal and Mr. Matthews stood up on either side of Mr. Ricky.

"Kindly lead out thuh school board chairman – in – uh – accordance with section two hundred an' – uh – sixty – paragraft ten – which says – ennybuddy don't shet up when they're told three times, jist take 'em outa thuh hall."

"But there ain't enny such – "

I guess Mr. Ricky finished up outside.

I don't understand so well how they worked it, but Ma says Miss Henchbaw's staying. After the folks voted they asked Mr. Ricky to quit being chairman. He did. Even Mr. Ricky, Jake says, hadn't got the nerve to hang on after that meeting.

7

The Liar Hunter

IF THERE is anything folks are more fussy about than
their own kids, Jake says, it is the truth. They will get
pretty snuffy if someone tells them they haven't got any
too good a grip on the truth. Jake ought to know; sometimes he will give the truth a stretch or two, but not like
Old Man Gatenby. When Jake is done with her she will
snap back into place; with Old Gate she is stretched for
good.

Old Man Gatenby lives on his half section down Government Road from us, him and his daughter, Molly. He is
about 40% wheat farmer, Jake says, 30% plain liar, and
30% magnifying glass. Even so, folks don't call him a liar.
Not with the temper he's got.

Truth is a real handy thing to have lying around, Jake
says, but sometimes a little of her will go a long ways. Miss
Henchbaw at Rabbit Hill says Jake makes too little go too
long a ways. You would expect her to say that. She is a

teacher. She wouldn't be so fussy about the truth if she had got mixed up with Mr. Godfrey last summer.

Mr. Godfrey was the fellow came out West to visit with Molly Gatenby, and it was him gave Old Gate the worst dose of the truth that he ever got. Jake and me saw him the first day he was in town, because Old Man Gatenby was busy finishing up his crop and he asked us to give Mr. Godfrey a lift out from town. We did.

Without those glasses and that pale sort of a skin he had he would have been a nice-looking fellow. His eyes put me in mind of Mr. Cameron's when he goes on about the flesh being so awful and the spirit being so dandy – dark and burny. Whenever he would say anything the words came out real far apart, like flies he was picking off fly-paper. He was all the time clearing his throat just before he said something. He could have been a consolidated school principal.

He was just the kind of a fellow you would expect Molly to run with, her being so schoolteacher serious too. It is funny for Old Gate to have a daughter like Molly. Her eyes are not old-timer eyes. Her face is not all creased up like some brown paper you crumple in your hand and then try to smooth out. Her eyes will put you in mind of those violets that are tangled up in prairie grass along about the end of April.

I guess she is the violet and Old Gate is the dead grass. That's how they are.

Until we were out of Crocus, with Baldy's hind quarters tipping up and down real regular and telephone poles stretching clear to the horizon, Mr. Godfrey didn't say anything. Then he cleared his throat and said:

"The smallness of man – the prairies bring it to one with – such impact – it – is almost the catharsis of tragedy."

A jack rabbit started up to the left of the road, went over the prairie in a sailing bounce. "Huh!" Jake said.

"Catharsis – cleansing – as in the Greek tragedy – cathartic."

"Oh," Jake said, "that. Thuh alkali water sure is fear . . ."

"Oh, no," Mr. Godfrey said. "I mean that it – has a . . ."

"Prairie's scarey," I said.

"Yes." He looked down at me. "That's it – exactly it."

"I heard yuh was one of them prefessers," Jake said. He spit curvy into the breeze. "Ain't diggin' in thuh bank of thuh Brokenshell, are yuh?" He meant where they're getting those bones – the big ones that are older than anything.

"I dig," Mr. Godfrey said, "in a manner of speaking – but for folklore."

"Whut kinda ore?"

"Lore. Folklore – art – the common people . . ."

"That's real nice." Jake jiggled the lines at Baldy's rump. "Who the heck is Art an' what's this all about?"

"Why – I . . ." He cleared his throat. "I look for songs – ballads that have – that express the life of the Old West."

" 'Baggage Coach Behin' the Train'?" Jake said. " 'Where Do the Flies Go in the Wintertime?' "

"But – mostly stories," Mr. Godfrey said, "tall tales."

"Is that right?" Jake looked real pleased, and he cleared his throat the way he does before he starts to yarn.

"I'm looking for liars," Mr. Godfrey said.

Those dark, hungry eyes were staring right at Jake.

Jake swallowed. "Yuh don't hafta look at me!"

"Sorry."

"You bin talkin' to Miss Henchbaw!"

"Do you think that she might help me? . . ."

"Her! Truthfullest woman we got aroun' here – next tuh Molly Gatenby. Why, she . . ."

"Would you consider Mr. Gatenby a good source – of tall tales?"

"All depends," Jake said. "Anythin' Gate tells yuh, she's

blowed up to about four times natural size. You take hail-stones – "

"A chronic liar."

"Say!" Jake jumped. "Jist who do you – oh – yuh mean Gate."

"Interesting type."

"How many kindsa liars you turned up so far?"

"There's the defensive liar – and the occasional liar. I mentioned the chronic liar. The pragmatic or practical liar. I'm looking for the creative liar, of course."

"Oh – a-course," Jake said. "About Gate – I wouldn't like tuh say he lied exactly – jist sorta deckerates thuh truth a bit." He looked away from Mr. Godfrey's eyes. "That's all." He looked back to Mr. Godfrey. "Tell me somethin'. You ever run intuh any trouble with folks?"

"Not yet," said Mr. Godfrey.

"Well, young fella," Jake said, "ye're gonna."

The rest of the way home we just rolled along with the buckboard wheels sort of grinding. A gopher squeaked a couple of times. The way it is in fall, the air was just like soda pop. Every once in a while would come a tickle to your nose or your forehead, and you would brush at it, only it would keep right on tickling. You couldn't see the spider webs floating on the air, except where sunshine caught onto them and slid down. Mr. Godfrey had a lost look on his face whilst he stared off to the horizon with its straw-stacks curling their smoke into the soft blue sky.

At Gatenby's corner Mr. Godfrey said thanks very much, and Jake looked like he was going to say something, then he seemed to change his mind and clucked at Baldy in-stead. Just before we turned in, Jake said: "I kin har'ly wait fer Gate tuh come over fer rummy tuhmorra night."

But Old Gate didn't come till a week later, and when he got to our place he wasn't joking about how he'd nail Jake's hide to a fence post. All the time he played rummy he kept drumming his fingers on the kitchen table. I saw him miss the Queen of Hearts for a run and the ten of spades to make up three of a kind. Jake marked down 45 against Gate.

"Ain't doin' so smart tuhnight, Gate."

"Deal them there cards."

"Yore deal, Gate."

Gate started in shuffling the cards, all the time chewing so his chin come up almost to his nose.

Jake picked up the first card Gate dealt. "Looks like a early winter."

"Leave them cards lie till I git 'em dealt!" Gate said it real short. Then, " 'Tain't polite."

Jake didn't say anything at all.

Gate lost the whole game. When Jake shoved him the cards to deal a new hand, he said:

"Tuh hell with her, Jake."

"Ain't yuh feelin' so good, Gate?"

"Feelin' good!" Gate's voice cracked. He leaned across the table. "Right now you are lookin' a teetotal nervous wreck right between the eyes!"

"Now – that's too – "

"My nerves – plum onstrung – hangin' lose as thuh fringe on a Indian jacket. I tripped in 'em three times yesterday between thuh hog pens an' thuh stock trough. An – "

"I wouldn't take on like that, Gate," Jake said. "Yuh gotta relax."

"Take on! Relax! 'Tain't no skin offa yore knuckles! 'Tain't you she's callin' a liar – in yer own house – in fronta yer own daughter!"

Jake's mouth dropped open. "Did he do that, Gate?"

"He might as well an' be done with her!"

"Either he did," Jake said, "er he didn't. Whatta yuh mean?"

"Look," Mr. Gatenby said, "he's got him a little black notebook – keeps her in his hip pocket – every time I open

my mouth, he opens that there notebook! ' 'Member thuh
winter of o' six,' I sez. Out comes thuh notebook. 'Is it a
fact?' he sez. 'Certain'y is,' I sez. Bang, he snaps her shet
– me too. Can't git another word outa me! Like thrashin' –
ready tuh roll an' he ups an' throws a ball of binder twine
intuh thuh cylinders. 'Is it a fact?' he sez. Whut's he think
I'm gonna tell him, thuh fat-brained, stoop-shouldered – "

"Now – ain't that cathartic."

Old Gate stared at Jake.

"New way of sayin' she's tragical," Jake said quick.

Gate grunted. "I'll tell yuh one thing fer certain – they
ain't gonna be no liar hunters tied up with thuh Gatenby
outfit."

He meant it.

A couple of nights later I heard Ma and my Aunt
Margaret talking whilst they were giving the baby his bath.
Aunt Margaret stays with us whilst her husband is in the
Navy. My dad fights too; he fights for the South Saskat-
chewans. It is Aunt Margaret's baby.

I heard her say, "With Herbert gathering this folklore,
she's ashamed of her own father."

"Ashamed of her father!" Ma said.

"I hope nothing comes of it," Aunt Margaret said. "It
would – "

"You can let his head back now." Ma looked at Aunt
Margaret whilst she wrung out the washcloth. "Molly's nobody's fool. Her heart isn't going to break in a hurry. In
many ways she's her father's daughter."

"A liar, Ma?"

"She is not! Don't you dare use that word again! That
wood box – "

"I already filled it."

"Help Jake with the cream then."

I told Jake all about it. I said, "There's a dustup coming
over to Gatenby's, Jake."

"Is there, now?" Jake said.

"Molly isn't so fussy about Mr. Godfrey makin' out her father's a – a – what he's makin' him out to be."

"A tradegy," Jake said, "to give a Greek thuh heart-burn."

But a week later Jake was laughing on the other side of his face, when the whole works came over to our place to visit. That was the night Mr. Godfrey said something about how hot it had been down East that summer.

"Hot here too," Jake said. For a minute he worked on his teeth with a sharpened matchstick and then he said. "Take thuh second week in July – tar paper on thuh roof of thuh chicken house – she all bubbled up."

"Did it really?" said Mr. Godfrey. On the chair beside him was Molly, sitting straight up like she expected something to happen, and she wanted to be ready to take off quick. Old Gate he'd hardly said anything since they came, just stared at the gas lamp in the centre of the kitchen table.

"Bubbled right up," Jake said. "Noon of thuh second day, wispy sorta smoke was coming off of her."

"That a fact?"

Jake gave a little start like he'd stuck himself with the point of the matchstick. "Why – certain'y," he said.

"Herbert – please!" Molly said it the way Ma talks when she's holding in before company. I took a good look at her then, and I couldn't see where she was like Old Gate. Take her hair in that lamplight, real pretty – yellow as a straw-stack with the sun lying on it. Take her mouth, the way it is so red; take her all around she is pretty as a sorrel colt. Gate is enough to give a gopher the heartburn.

" – a hawin' an' a cawin' jist as I come out," Jake was saying. "That there tar paper on thuh hen house roof was so sticky thuh dumb fool crow had got himself stuck up in it. Real comical he was – liftin' one foot an' then thuh other. Course she was kinda tragical too – that there tar was hot. Musta bin kinda painful."

"Why – that's a wonderful – "

Molly cleared her throat, sort of warning; Mr. Godfrey quit reaching for his hip pocket.

"Inside of 10 minnits," Jake went on, "a whole flocka crows was circlin' over, the way they will when they hear another in trouble, an' buhfore I knew it thuh whole roof was stuck up with crows somethin' fearful."

"Herbert!" Mr. Godfrey had his notebook out and was opening it on his knee. He didn't pay any attention to Molly and the funny look she had on her face.

"Aflutterin' an' ahollerin', with their wings aslapping – our hen house sort of liftin' an' then settlin' back agin. I headed fer thuh woodpile."

"What for, Jake?" I said.

"Axe – wasn't gonna let that hen house go without a fight. I chopped thuh roof loose from thuh uprights an' away she went. Cleared thuh peak of thuh barn an' headed south."

Molly was standing up and she was looking down at Mr. Godfrey writing away like anything. Her face looked kind of white to me. "It's about time we were going," she said real soft.

"But we've just come!" Mr. Godfrey said. "This is the sort of thing I – "

"Folklore!" Molly said it like a cuss word.

Mr. Godfrey smiled and nodded his head and turned to Jake. "How long after the first crow came did – "

"Let her go fer tuhnight," Jake said.

"Don't look now," Molly said with her voice tight, "but I'm tired and sick of being Exhibit A for the common people. Any time you feel you can – "

"Oh, no, Molly," Mr. Godfrey said, "you don't und – "

"I'm afraid I do. These happen to be my people. They – "

"No call tuh fly off of thuh handle," Jake told her.

"A little more tact on your part, Jake, wouldn't have hurt at all!"

"Me – I didn't do nothin'. That there story – "

"Just a tall tale," Molly cut in on him, "like the thousands I've listened to all my life. I'm funny, but – "

"You shore are!" Jake said.

"There isn't any harm in them." Ma said.

"What makes it worse," Molly said, "is they have no – no point – useless – utterly senseless and – immoral!"

"I can explain what it is that – " Mr. Godfrey began.

"You've been our guest!" Molly turned on him. "Not for one minute have you stopped insinuating that my – "

"I haven't been making any – "

"You certainly have!"

"Will you let me explain?"

"It's a little late for that!"

"It shore is!" Jake was mad. "Standin' there on yer hind feet an' sayin' I'm senseless an' useless an – an' im – immortal!"

"Please, Jake." That was Ma.

I got a look at Gate, and he had a grin clear across his face.

"That story about them – "

"Was a lie, Jake Trumper! However you want – "

"Are you callin' me a liar?" Jake he was off of the wood box.

"I hate to do it," Molly said, "but you asked for it, Jake. You are the biggest . . . two-handed . . . clod-busting liar I have ever known!"

The kitchen clock ticked real loud against the silence. I could hear Jake's breath whistling in his nose.

"With one exception," Molly said. "My dad." She turned to Old Gate. "Take me home!"

I knew then what Ma meant; she is Gate's daughter all right. I felt kind of sorry for Mr. Godfrey.

I felt even more sorry for him the day me and Jake went into Crocus for Ma's groceries. He was standing beside some yellow suitcases inside of MacTaggart's, right by the door. Halfway down the counter was Molly; she stayed there.

"Hullo," Jake said. "You catchin' thuh four-ten?"

"Yes," Mr. Godfrey said.

"Sorry tuh see yuh go."

"You're alone in your sentiment."

"Huh?"

"I say – you're the only one who is."

"Oh – I wouldn't – "

"I would," Mr. Godfrey said. "I've made a mess of things, and there's no use pretending I haven't." He was staring at Jake that way I told you about. I sort of fiddled with a double-oh gopher trap hanging down from the counter. Mr. Godfrey looked past Jake to Molly by the canned tomatoes. She turned away. "I'd like to tell you something before I go."

"Shoot," Jake said.

"Somethin' fer yuh tuhday?" That was Mr. MacTaggart, who had come out from the back and was leaning across the counter to Molly.

"My work is important," Mr. Godfrey said. "I'm not just a – a liar hunter simply." He was real serious. He wasn't looking at Jake.

"Any apples in?" Molly said.

"Apples," Mr. MacTaggart said, and wrote it down with his stubby pencil, then looked up at Molly for what was next.

"What I do is important. Important as history is important." Mr. Godfrey wasn't dropping his words in relays now, but talking straight along, maybe because he was so darn serious.

"Gee!" I said, "you should hear how Jake wrassled Looie Riel an' – "

"Hold her, Kid!"

"Not the history of great and famous men," Mr. Godfrey explained, "but of the lumberjacks and section men, hotel-keepers and teachers and ranchers and farmers. The people that really count."

"And – a tin of blackstrap," Molly said it to Mr. Mac-Taggart, but she was looking at Mr. Godfrey. She didn't sound like she was so fussy about getting any molasses.

"Their history isn't to be found in records or in books."

"This here Ontario cheese is real nice."

"Their history is in the stories they tell – their tall tales. That's why I gather – "

"Good an' nippy."

"And a pound of cheese," Molly said.

"And I can tell you why they lie," Mr. Godfrey said.

"Anythin' else?" Mr. MacTaggart said.

"If you're interested," Mr. Godfrey said.

"That'll be nice," Jake said.

"Was there somethin' else?" Mr. MacTaggart asked.

"This is a hard country, I don't have to tell you that. There are – drouth, blizzards, loneliness. A man is a pretty small thing out on all this prairie. He is at the mercy of the elements. He's a lot like – like a – "

"Fly on a platter," I said.

"Was there somethin' else yuh wanted?" said Mr. Mac-Taggart.

"That's right," Mr. Godfrey said. "These men lie about the things that hurt them most. Their yarns are about the winters and how cold they are the summers and how dry they are. In this country you get the deepest snow, the worst dust storms, the biggest hailstones."

"Mebbe yuh didn't hear me – " Mr. MacTaggart said to Molly – "Was there somethin' more yuh wanted?"

"Rust and dust and hail and sawfly and cutworm and drouth are terrible things, but not half as frightening if they are made ridiculous. If a man can laugh at them he's won half the battle. When he exaggerates things he isn't lying really; it's a defence, the defence of exaggeration. He can either do that or squeal." Mr. Godfrey picked up his bags and started for the door.

"Whilst you stand there makin' up yer mind," Mr. Mac-Taggart said, "I'll get tuh Mrs. Totcoal's order."

"People in this country aren't squealers." Mr. Godfrey was standing in the doorway.

"You go ahead with the Totcoal order," Molly said to Mr. MacTaggart with her eyes on Mr. Godfrey. She walked right up to him and she looked right at him. "I think I've just made up my mind."

"Hey!" yelled Mr. MacTaggart, "not right in front of – "

"Jist a new kinda hist'ry," Jake said, "gonna tickle Old Gate right up the back."

"Oh!" Molly turned around. "I'd – what are we – what about Dad! He said if Herbert ever – "

"Mr. Godfrey better come out with us," Jake said. "Don't you tell yer paw anythin' about him still bein' here. Jist say ye're invited over to our place fer tuhnight. I got me a notion." Jake leaned down and picked up Mr. Godfrey's bags. "I got me a notion about what makes Old Gate tick."

At our barn Jake told me to beat it and I did. Him and Mr. Godfrey were in there for quite a while. Me, I was wondering what made Old Man Gatenby tick. I didn't find out till that night.

Gate got quite a start when he saw Mr. Godfrey.

"Ain't you went yet?" he said.

"I – I missed the train," Mr. Godfrey said. That was his first lie, what you might call a warming-up lie. Molly's face got kind of red. Gate he settled back in his chair like he was ready for a tough evening.

"Never fergit thuh year hoppers was so bad," Jake said. "Blacked out thuh sun complete."

"This district had them terribly, I understand," Mr. Godfrey said. "Of course they weren't so big, were they?"

"Big!" Jake said. "One of 'em lit on thuh airport at Broomhead an' a RAF fella run 100 gallons a gas intuh him afore he reelized – "

"Albin!" Mr. Godfrey said – "Albin Hobblemeyer, they called that grasshopper. I have him in my files. Three years ago he – "

"Is that a fact?" Jake said.

"They named him as soon as he set foot in the district, after a man named Hobblemeyer – squashed him to death. Matter of fact he's upset a number of the investigators digging for prehistoric remains in the bank of the Brokenshell. They're not so sure that – "

"Yuh mean – mebbe them Brokenshell bones belonged to the great great gran'daddies of that there hopper?" Jake said.

"He was that big," Mr. Godfrey said. "When he leaped, the back lash from his shanks licked up the topsoil for miles behind him and the tumbleweeds – "

"Say – " Old Gate was on the edge of his chair.

"He spit tobacco juice and smeared over an entire schoolhouse just newly painted. Naturally he caused a lot of excitement. People were worried sick. They couldn't destroy him – bullets, buckshot just bounced off his chitinous hide, and people began to wonder what it would be like when he – "

"That's a pretty feeble – " Gate started in.

" – began to lay eggs. They decided the only thing they could do would be to keep it on the hop."

"Why, Mr. Godfrey?" I asked.

"A grasshopper has to dig a hole and back into it before it can lay. It was unfortunate that there was a man in the district named – uh – "

"Dewdney," Jake said. "Wasn't there a fella name of – " Gate, he had a funny look on his face, like a fellow wanting a swim real bad but not wanting to take the jump. "Ain't no fella name a Dewdney in Broomhead. There's Dooley – got one leg shorter than thuh other – one-an'-a-half-step Dooley."

"That was the man," Mr. Godfrey said, and Old Gate looked startled. "A very close man who had wanted to dig himself a reservoir to catch the spring run-off and couldn't bring himself to laying out the money it would cost. He couldn't resist the temptation to let the grasshopper dig it for him."

Gate's mouth dropped open and stayed that way.

"Unfortunately," Mr. Godfrey said, "Albin laid an egg."

Gate swallowed. "Tell me," he said, "jist – how – how big an egg would a hopper like that lay?"

"Quite round," Mr. Godfrey said, "and about the size of the average chicken house. Mr. – uh – "

"Dooley," Gate said kind of dazed.

" – he tried to crack it with an axe, and succeeded only in throwing his right shoulder out of joint when the axe bounced off the egg."

"I'll be – "

"He decided then to pile birch chunks around it and in that way – uh – fry it – so that it couldn't hatch. As soon as he had the wood lighted he got frantic as he thought that perhaps the heat might only speed up the hatching. So he put the fire out."

"What thuh hell did he do?" Old Gate was really interested now.

"He rounded up the district's entire supply of stumping powder. The last seen of the egg, it was headed for the States."

Old Gate's breath came out of him in one long swoosh.

"Is – that – a – fact?" He said it real weak.

Mr. Godfrey was looking over at Molly, and she was smiling. Jake looked like he'd just thrashed a 60-bushel crop, too.

It was a week later, after Mr. Godfrey had gone back to stay with Gatenbys, that I asked Jake about something that had bothered me ever since that night.

"Jake," I said, "he never told what happened to that hopper."

"There," Jake said, "is thuh tragical part of it. Albin, he fell in love."

"Fell in love!"

"Yep. He was settin' in this here Dooley's back 40 one day an' he looked up an' seen one a them there four-engine bombers they're flyin' tuh Roosia. She was love at first sight. He took off, an' thuh last folks seen was two little black specks disappearin' tuh thuh North. Han' me that there manure fork will yuh, Kid?"

8

Auction Fever

I HAD the measles and the prairie itch once and the mumps on both sides. I had the black crowing, Ma says, but I never had the worst of all. Jake says it often hits our district, sometimes in the spring and sometimes in the fall; it knocks folks over like the disease that runs through jack rabbits every seven years: Auction fever.

A lot of folks must have figured it got Jake this spring, but that wasn't auction fever at all; that was the Duke of Broomhead. A person couldn't say Jake caught auction fever off of a snuffy York boar, could they? If the Duke of Broomhead hadn't bit Jake between the household goods and the red weeder, we would have had lots of money left over for the little buckskin colt. You'll see what I mean, later.

Colonel Hepworth held the sale in back of Hig Wheeler's lumberyard, where it says, "We built the West." "Hup-an'-a-whiddle-eeee-diddle-ho-riddle-hum – who'll bid me five an' a five an' a five?" There is the way Colonel Hepworth sells stuff for folks. He is a long thin fellow with the build of a Kentucky whip; he has a long, thin horse face too, and he wears a coat with a velvet collar, and a bowler hat. He waves a cane around all the time. He makes the folks laugh a lot.

Ma gave Jake fifty dollars to buy her a stove; she didn't come into Crocus with us; she knows Jake is a good trader. Jake says once he started out with only a cotter pin and he ended up with a burning harrow, a bull calf, and ten dollars to boot; he did it in thirty-one trades. That will show you.

At the sale we ran across all kinds of folks from our district, all of them with stuff hanging out of their hands: slop pails, picture frames, lanterns, disk plates, bridles. Old Man Gatenby he had a lamp under one arm; the shade was shaped like a long haystack, only you don't see many pink haystacks with tassels hanging around them. I better not say what he had under his other arm.

Jake asked him where was the stove at, because Ma's grate had burned out. He said over behind the implements.

It is bad enough in spring with the air sort of soft and sweet and you feel lazy in your knees; but with an auction sale besides, it is no wonder folks feel like kicking over the britching.

Kids were playing tag all around their folks' legs; the cows and calves were bawling, and the chickens in their crates were cut-cutting to beat anything. We could hear Colonel Hepworth's voice coming floaty to us: "Huppy-oh-whiddle-eeee-diddle-hoo-a ten an' a ten, but what I want is fifteen!" Like a circus. Just like a circus.

"Holy diddle!" Jake had a look on his face like he didn't believe what he saw. "Thinka anybuddy havin' a shaganappy thing like that in their house!"

One of her legs was off, so she leaned to one side like a horse resting on a hot day; she was all scuffed up and carved up and battered up. Springs hung out of her bottom;

they were poking out her top. I guess she was a couch.

Jake bent down for a closer look. Her back was curved out in two places, just about right to catch a person between the shoulder blades. Along the front were baby angels with their cheeks blown out, and in the middle of the top were two black hawks. They must have been mad at each other, because they were pointed in the opposite direction.

Jake straightened up and he had a look on his face like his gums were hurting him. "Ain't that enuff tuh give a badger thuh heartburn!" he said. "Pore thing ain't ever had a chance tuh heal up!"

"What is it, Jake?"

"Search me," Jake said. "Could call her a gosh-hawk couch, I guess."

That was when Jake saw the stove over by the cream separator. While he looked inside her, I headed for the stock pens.

Then I saw the colt.

I don't even remember climbing up to sit on the rail of his pen. All I know is that I was up there with my toes hooked around the rail, and I was looking down on that colt, soaking him in, his shaggy coat the colour of pull taffy, his silver mane and tail, and his hoofs just like Ma's teacups.

I never said to myself, I want him. It was quicker than thinking, quick as a gopher down a hole. I wanted him so bad I hurt, the funny kind when you can't tell where you hurt but you sure know you do.

I could feel the spring chinook soft at my nose and hear it in my ears. It was whispering in the long grass at the side of the pen! It had come clear across the prairie to me and my buckskin colt.

I got down off of that fence and I headed for Jake. He knows what to get for a kid.

I found him on the edge of all the folks ringed around Colonel Hepworth and looking up at him.

"Jake!" I said. "I just been over to the stock pens and I saw a buckskin colt!"

"Did yuh now?"

"He's a buckskin, Jake, I'd like for you to look at him – he's a buckskin with a real light mane and a tail!"

"Look kinda funny without one," Jake said. "There ain't no – "

" – sold to thuh fella in thuh trainman's cap!" yelled Colonel Hepworth. "An' now, gen'lemen, let us turn to thuh pigs!"

" – jist talkin' about it thuh other day. Yer maw figgers it's about time fer yuh to have a horse-a yer own." Jake had a real pleased look on his face. "Got yer maw's stove – Pride-a the Prairies – hot-water ressy-voar on her – on'y thirty dollars – leaves twen'y left over."

"Jake, do you think – could – I want that there colt, Jake – I want – "

"Ain't no harm in takin' a look at him," Jake said.

Whilst Jake looked at the colt I stood there and hoped like anything he would be all right so Jake would buy him.

"Risin' a year," Jake said. "Nice put-up colt."

"Can I – will you buy him for me, Jake?"

Jake spit. "I will," he said, "if he don't go over twenty."

"Do you think he – "

"Nope – I don't think he will. C'm'on – we'll stick close to thuh colonel till he gits tuh that there colt."

Colonel Hepworth was standing up on the seat of an old MacDougall tractor next to the hogpens. He was pointing to the Duke of Broomhead with his cane, and he had an envelope in his hand.

"This here pig, gen'lemen, is thuh Duke-a Broomhead – pure-blood registered York boar with a stringa folks from here tuh thuh correction line. Take a look at that there royal pig!"

I could see the Duke of Broomhead's angry little eyes

looking out between the rails of his pen. He was chomping and breathing real mad. I took a couple of steps back from the pen. Jake didn't. Jake isn't scared of anything.

"Now whut am I bid fer this here pig, gen'lemen – hup – let her go – huppa-diddle-eee-hi-widdle-ho – thanks for thuh five-dollar bid – thuh ree-dickalus sum-a five dollars fer – who'll gimme ten – an' a ten an' a ten – ten I am give!"

I didn't see anybody make a five- or a ten-dollar bid; a person doesn't dare spit when Colonel Hepworth is selling.

"An' fifteen – five an' a ten an' a ten an' a five – an' a huppy-eye-oh-ring-a-dang-doh! Fifteen ain't enuff – my heart bleeds fer the pig a-holdin' his noble head low in shame – blue blood, gen'lemen, blue as the ink in yer fountain pen, gen'lemen!"

"Lard!" Jake snorted.

"Lard, Jake?"

"All he's good for – that's a five-year-old boar – too old – he ain't no good for – "

"Who'll gimme two more – more – two more – fifteen an' a two – "

"Then what are they bidding for, Jake?"

"Auction fever, Kid – that pig ain't worth thuh haulin' away."

"One dollar is all I ask – one dollar more tuh save that there pig's pride – huppy-oh-whiddle-eeee-rum – don't nobody feel sorry fer that there pig?"

Jake was leaning against the Duke of Broomhead's pen with his elbow on the top rail.

"Thuh papers ain't extra!" yelled Colonel Hepworth waving the envelope around. "All fer thuh price-a fifteen dollars – fifteen once an' a fifteen twice – who'll bid me fifty cents more – four bits more – "

"Hey – ow – uh!" Just like the four-ten on a clear fall night, Jake let a whoop out of him and jumped like a startled jack rabbit.

Colonel Hepworth's cane came down with a bang. "Sold!" he shouted. "Sold tuh Jake Trumper fer fifteen an' a half – an' a very fine buy you've – "

Jake quit dancing around with his hand on the back of his leg.

"Hey – wait a minnit – I ain't bought nothin'! I didn't bid on no worn-out – "

"Thuh bid wuz made an' Pete's a-markin' her down – cash bag's to yer right. Now, gen'lemen, let us turn tuh – "

"You ain't gonna stick me with – " Jake had quit rubbing the seat of his overalls. "That there damn boar jist tooka chunk outa my – "

"Terms is strickly cash," said Colonel Hepworth. "You wouldn't be tryin' tuh back out, would yuh?"

"No, I ain't," said Jake; "I'm jist tryin' tuh tell yuh I – "

"If yuh ain't satisfied, yuh kin put him up fer rebiddin'."

"But I didn't bid in thuh first pl – "

"Yuh want him up ag'in?"

"Hell, no! He ain't even mine!"

"He sure is! Make up yer mind – we ain't got all day – there's a lotta stuff tuh go yet. Thuh steers is next. Yes er no?"

Jake he looked sort of helpless and mad at the same time. He jerked his head up and down. He was too mad to talk.

The Duke of Broomhead sold to Magnus Petersen for five dollars.

Whilst Jake collected five dollars off of Magnus and forked out fifteen fifty to Pete Stover, I thought about my little buckskin colt. I thought about the sunlight on the real fine hairs bearding under his chin and the wind lifting his woolly tail. I didn't feel so good. Ten fifty from twenty is nine fifty. That won't buy any colt.

"Nine fifty isn't enough for any colt, Jake!"

Jake looked down at me and he said, "I'm sorry, Kid." That was all he said. Me, I could feel my arm around that colt's neck, and my throat started to get all plugged up.

"But – can't – couldn't – "

"Ain't nothin' we kin do, Kid. Yuh heard him say – she's strick'ly cash."

"Couldn't we go downtown an' – "

"Ain't no time fer that," Jake said. He looked down at the nine fifty he had in his hand.

"Could we trade around a little, Jake, and – like that there cotter – "

"He's startin' on them cows an' steers – "

"Couldn't we trade around – "

"Huh?"

"I said – couldn't we trade around, the way you did when you ended up with the – "

Jake stared at me. "We might," he said. "Nine fifty – that there colt might go at twen'y. Kid, we're gonna haftuh work fast. We – Hey, Johnny!"

That was Johnny Totcoal, and he was carrying a big moose's head.

"You got papers fer him, Johnny?"

Johnny was looking kind of disgusted. "Missus is gonna snatch me bald-headed when she sees this here critter."

"Why did yuh buy him for?"

"I dunno – jist seemed like a real good buy at eight fifty."

"Was yuh wantin' tuh sell him – "

"I sure was."

"Whatta yuh want?"

"I'd kinda like tuh git what I paid fer him, Jake."

"He's missin' one eye, ain't he, Johnny?"

"I'd let him go fer seven fifty."

"Moths bin tuh work on that left ear."

"Seven dollars'd be a real good price on him," Johnny said.

"I might give yuh five."

"Make her six, Jake."

"Ain't that there stuffin' comin' outa his neck?"

"I'd be takin' a two-fifty loss."

"Give yuh five."

"Make her six, Jake."

"Five fifty."

"He's yores."

When Johnny had left, Jake turned to me. "Up fifty – down three – that's thuh way tuh do her, Kid."

It was Old Man Gatenby we ran into next, and Jake said to him, "When did yuh git thuh power line intuh yore place?"

"We ain't got her," Old Man Gatenby said.

"Looks like that there 'lectric lamp's gonna come in real handy," Jake said. "Gonna put in wind ee-lectric, are you?"

"Can't till after thuh war," Gate said.

"Well," Jake said, "she'll look nice anyways – even if yuh can't light her up."

"You wouldn't be int'rested, would yuh?"

"Hell, no – we ain't got ee-lectricity neither. Fella's gotta be real careful round a auction, Gate. Take me – I come here fer one thing – jist one thing – this here gen-you-wine moose's head – I got him."

Gate set his lamp down on the ground and he stared at the moose's head, and he scratched his jaw slow like your nail on sandpaper. "Wut thuh hell fer?"

"Why, deckeration," Jake said. "He's gonna look real nice up on thuh wall – over thuh fireplace. Go real nice over a fella's fireplace, wouldn't he?"

"He might," Old Man Gatenby said.

"Kinda keep a fella comp'ny, I figger."

"Ummm," said Old Man Gatenby.

"Too bad about that there lamp, Gate."

"Yeah – uh – don't wanta make a trade, do yuh?"

"Nope," Jake said. "We ain't got ee – "

"Give yuh two dollars tuh boot," said Gate.

Jake didn't even say yes. He dropped the moose's head and he grabbed that lamp. Gate gave him two dollars, and we started off.

"Hey!" yelled Gate. "I jist remembered – I ain't got no fireplace neither!"

We kept right on going.

Mrs. Biggs was standing beside a washtub, two slop pails, a bed spring, and a brass bedstead.

"Nice day," Jake said with his eye on the bed.

"Cer'n'y is," Mrs. Biggs said. She lives in town.

"Nice crowd," Jake said.

"Cer'n'y is," Mrs. Biggs said.

"Nice lamp here," Jake said.

"Cer'n'y is," Mrs. Biggs said.

"Go real nice with alla that lovely furniture-a yores," Jake said.

" 'T might," said Mrs. Biggs.

"Nice bedstead yuh got there, Mrs. Biggs."

" 'T ain't what I told Charlie tuh git," she said. "I told him a Winnipeg couch fer when Florence come tuh stay with us, an' he went an' – "

"P'r'aps yuh could use this here lamp better," said Jake. "She's double-lined silk, yuh know – quit makin' 'em sence thuh war."

I looked at the lamp, and I was wondering did Jake mean the last war or the Boer War. And then I wasn't caring about any lamp, because I could hear Colonel Hepworth yelling, "Hup – an' this's thuh lasta thuh cows – " I started in thinking how that colt's nose would be real velvet against a person's neck, and I was thinking how I always was fussy about a horse with a white blaze in the middle of his forehead.

"C'm'on, Kid." Jake had one end of the bedstead, and he wanted for me to help him haul her off a ways. Over by our wagon box, Jake counted up our money. He'd given two dollars to boot for the bed; that left four dollars.

"She's worth about fifteen bucks," Jake said. "We're gittin' within strikin' distance-a that colt."

"But, Jake, he's finishin' up the cows already!"

"I know it. All we gotta do is find somebuddy wants a bed an' – "

"Just whut I'm lookin' fer."

Jake and me turned. It was Mr. Ricky. Nobody gets the best of Mr. Ricky.

"Yuh wanta buy a bed?" Jake said.

"Shore do," said Mr. Ricky. "Not buy exac'ly – figgered tuh trade."

"Yuh kin have her fer sixteen dollars," Jake said.

Mr. Ricky shook his head. "Give yuh six dollars an' a dye-van."

"A whut!"

"A dye-van – high-class piece-a furniture. Mind yuh, she ain't A-one."

"Whut is it?"

"A sorta chesterfield – ain't new – kinda scuffed up some – "

"Jake! He's startin' in on the colt – he's sellin' – "

"Springs is all there. I paid twelve dollars fer her."

"Where is she?"

"I ain't got thuh time ner thuh energy tuh take yuh over – I tell yuh she's a good trade – six dollars tuh boot."

"I'd like tuh see her first," Jake said.

"We haven't got time, Jake!"

" – five I am bid an' that don't nearly pay thuh stud fee alone on this here colt – hup – look at him, gen'lemen – right next door tuh a Palomino – five an' a five. Who'll gimme ten?"

"Hurry, Jake."

"O. K.," Jake said.

Mr. Ricky handed him six dollars.

We ran for the other corner of the lot where Mr. Ricky said the thing was. And then we saw it.

Jake had traded us right into the gosh-hawk couch.

I felt kind of sick. Jake didn't look so good either. He said:

"Jist goes tuh show, Kid. When yuh trade, take yer time. Take – yer – damn – time!"

"But – what can we – "

"Here." Jake handed me our ten dollars. "You git over there an' start biddin' on that there colt. I'll see what I kin do about this here couch. Day, Mrs. Fotheringham."

That was Mrs. Fotheringham. She is married to Dr. Fotheringham. Her chest sticks out like on some pigeons.

"You haven't seen the doctor, have you?" she said to Jake.

"No, I ain't, Mrs. Fotheringham," Jake said.

"Hup – an' I got six fifty – six fifty bid for the colt – hup – gimme eight – an' eight an' eight – "

"Seven!" I yelled and I hadn't reached the edge of the crowd.

"Huppy-oh-seven I got – seven an' I asked fer eight – eight ain't enuff fer that blocky little colt. Who'll gimme eight? Who'll gimme eight? Eight I got – eight fer thuh colt."

"Eight an' twen'y-five cents!" I yelled.

"Two bits from thuh kid that wants that colt – two bits from the boy with the freckles on his nose – eight twen'y-five!"

"Nine!"

It was Mr. Ricky bidding against me. He knows a good thing when he sees it. Mr. Ricky sold us the gosh-hawk couch.

"Nine an' a quarter!" I shouted.

"An' a quarter from thuh two-bit kid – hup another bid – hup – gimme ten – "

Mr. Ricky nodded.

"Ten I got. Ten is all I got, an' thuh colt's worth thirty. If she goes fer a cent under thirty, I'll never sell another horse!"

"Twelve!" That was me did that, and I didn't care if I didn't have the money to pay. Mr. Ricky wasn't going to get my buckskin colt. That is the way auction fever gets a person.

"Fifteen!"

"Now we're comin' fine, gen'lemen – fifteen – five an' a ten an' a ten an' a five – five more fer thuh colt – five more fer – "

"Twenty!" That was me again with ten dollars in my pocket.

"Twen'y-one." Mr. Ricky didn't sound so anxious. Like Jake said, that colt would go near twenty.

I didn't know what to do. All I knew was I didn't want to live any more if I didn't get my colt. But I couldn't say it; I couldn't say twenty-two.

"Twenty-two!"

"Another bidder – twen'y-two he's give me – twen'y-two dollars – huppy-eye-oh-diddle-riddle-eee-hum – who'll gim-me twen'y-five – five an' a twen'y – twen'y an' a five!"

It sure was a new bidder. It was Jake; I could tell his voice anywhere. Jake has sold the gosh-hawk couch. Jake is smart. Jake is the smartest there is!

"Twen'y-two once – twen'y-two twice – twen'y-two fer thuh third an' last time! Sold! Sold tuh Jake Trumper, owner-a thuh Duke-a Broomhead an' – "

"Not no more I ain't!"

He was standing over beside Pete Stover and the cash bag. I headed for Jake.

He was counting out the money for my colt, and when he was through counting he still had a handful of bills.

"Jake, where did you – what – "

"Thuh gosh-hawk couch, Kid. Gen-you-wine Eyetalyun carvin' – Renny-saunce – Eyetalyun walnut. Mrs. Fotheringham's bin waitin' forty years tuh git her han's on that there couch. Doc wuz supposed tuh git it fer her whilst she was at Auxill'ary. Reel valuable that there stuff, she said – seventy-five dollars' valuable."

"You mean we got – "

"Yore maw's stove an' thuh colt an' thuh fifty dollars we come with an' thirteen dollars tuh boot."

I didn't say anything. I just looked at my colt with his proud neck and the wind in his mane.

"Pretty fussy about that there colt, Kid?"

"Oh, Jake! – he – I got a name for him."

"Have you now?"

"Fever, Jake – Auction Fever."

9

A Deal's a Deal

I COULD hear our house cracking its knuckles once in a while, the way it does at night, and Jake snoring gentle and the wind in my window screen and the frogs in our slough sort of stitching the quiet. Prairie gets real still at night.

I didn't feel so good lying there in bed. I kept thinking about Auction Fever and the way he bunts you with his nose, the way he runs when you turn him loose, slick as the wind through the smooth-on barley field. Just looking at him with his taffy-coloured hide and his silver mane and tail will make your throat plug up. He is next door to a Palomino. No wonder Mr. Ricky bid against us at the sale.

Mr. Ricky is one of the long, skinny kind that has an Adam's apple. Jake, our hired man, is skinny too. I figure Jake was born skinny; Mr. Ricky he's so mean he got skinny.

A rooster in our henhouse let half a crow out of him,

then shut up. I kept right on thinking about Fever. I thought how upset Ma was when we brought him home from the auction sale in town. She wanted me to have a horse all right, but not a colt that wasn't even broke. She had in mind a nice gentle school pony, she said. "I want him to get to school and back in one piece, Jake." Ma comes from down East; she's scared of horses. She used to be a schoolteacher.

And there was another thing I got to thinking about – being scared. I lay there with the moonlight real pale through my window, and I commenced to think about the day me and Jake halter-broke Fever. Just thinking about it, I got sort of grasshoppery to my insides. I still got that lump on the right side of my eye. I never told Ma about my elbow.

It happened the summer after Jake got me Fever, June summer, with the prairie greener than anything. Walking home from Rabbit Hill school, I could feel the sun warm on the back of my neck. Sometimes a gopher would squeak, and once I saw a weasel with his long neck straight up and his ears round, like you get on toy critters.

When I climbed under the barbed wire at our place, Fever was there to meet me; he walked right alongside of me to the house.

The back screen on our house slapped; I saw Jake crossing the yard with that limpy way he has. Looking at Jake's face, you would think he was real old; it is all creasy and the stubble is grey.

"Bring him into the c'rral," Jake said to me. "Gotta git goin'."

"Sure, Jake," I said. He'd promised me at breakfast we were going to halter-break Fever after school. "What do you want me to – "

"Jist shut that there gate whilst I git the halter an' a rope. Yer maw's took the eggs into town – got the rest o' the afternoon to work on him – have him halter-broke by the time she gits back. Gotta take her real slow an' patient, Kid."

While Jake was tying the rope to the end of the halter shank, I commenced to think about what Stevie Kiziw said. "Stevie says he'll be mean, Jake. He says all buckskins are mean because they got Indian – "

"Some is," said Jake, handing me the end of the rope. "So's a lotta blacks an' magpies. Take a dally round that there set post with the rope. Colour ain't got a hell of a lot to do with it. Idea is to git him closter an' closter to that post till we kin tie the halter rope. Lotta humans is mean too – colour ain't got nothin' to do with that."

"Stevie's just jealous," I said.

"You watch him, Kid – keep an eye onto him so's he don't run over you."

As Jake slid the halter gentle over Fever's nose, Fever tossed his head once. He stood still while Jake snapped it. "Call him to you," said Jake as he took the end of the rope from me.

I called and Fever took a couple of steps. Jake pulled in the slack on the rope, and that was when Fever felt the halter. He reared up, came down, and took a run at the fence. Jake tightened the rope; made it fast and yelled for me to get out of the way. Fever hit the fence.

"Git!" Jake yelled.

I tripped on a rock and went flat. Fever had the rope tight and was fighting his head to beat anything. Just as I got up, he jumped again, batted his head hard against the set post. I could see his nostrils wide, his eyes wild and bloodshot. "He's going to hurt – !" I started to yell.

Like you turn a pancake on a frying-pan, Fever flipped himself over. Jake said later it was his head hit my face.

Next thing I heard was the sound of our kitchen pump, then I felt the dipper of water Jake had thrown in my face.

I was on top of the kitchen table. The side of my face was all numb.

"You all right, Kid?" Jake looked real anxious.

"Sure, Jake," I said. "Just kind of shaky. I – the side of my face sort of tingles. We don't have to tell Ma, do we?"

"Don't make no difference. You got a shiner comin' up the colour of a crocus. By the time yer maw gits home should be the size of a thrasher's appetite."

Ma really got the coal oil on her fire when she saw my eye. "I knew something like this would happen!" she told Jake.

"Jist a accident," Jake said. "He'll be all right."

"He might have broken his neck! He's the only son I've got and I'm not taking any chances – "

"I tell you he'll be all right."

"That horse is dangerous! Why, just today in MacTaggart's store, Mr. Ricky was saying – "

"Ricky! He'd give his right arm to git that – "

"Mr. Ricky told me he had just the sort of horse we needed – gentle – quiet. I – Jake – I'm afraid of the – of that colt – "

"Look," Jake said. "You don't have to worry about that horse. You worry about the kid – all this here talkin' around about horses bein' dangerous – gotta go ahead with it now – unless you want him to be afraid of horses," Jake looked at her, "like you are."

"All right," Ma said, "we'll see."

But you should have seen her face when she went out and saw Fever tied up to the post, when she saw him trembling and wet with sweat and his eyes wild white and his nostrils real red. I started in getting kind of scared myself.

Jake broke off his snoring for a minute, then took up again. I got out of bed and went to my window. She was a clear night with a high tiddlywink moon. The hogpens, chicken coop, stock trough, barn were grey in the moon-light. Way off on the prairie a coyote howled. There is a sad sound for you.

I never thought of Mr. Ricky again after Ma mentioned him the day we halter-broke Fever. After school I'd run home and work with Fever the way Jake told me to. I'd talk to him and pat him and then get him to take a step on the end of the halter. It only took a couple of days to get him leading dandy.

Then Jake and me sacked him with a sack on the end of a rope, throwing it over his back and drawing it across and over his head. He didn't like that at first, but he got so he didn't mind.

Ma saw him get snuffy when we put the saddle on his back. She stood there by the fence, and I heard her take in her breath quick when he ran at me. I ducked out of the way, and that was all he did. By suppertime we could take the saddle off and put it on all we liked.

Ma had a funny look on her face at supper: her mouth was tight across her face. She set down Jake's prunes in front of him and she said:

"I got in touch with Mr. Ricky this afternoon."

Jake looked up quick. The way I jumped, I knocked over my glass.

"That horse is wild," Ma said.

"He's doin' jist fine," Jake said. "The kid and the horse is doin' jist fine."

"All the same," Ma said, "Mr. Ricky is calling tomor-row."

When Ma gets that special kind of a voice you know she used to be a schoolteacher.

Mr. Ricky he came the next day. I was with Jake at the hogpens when he came through our gate down by the wind-break. He was leading a horse.

"Look, Jake," I said.

Jake set down the two buckets he had; he watched Mr.

Ricky coming towards us. The horse was a real high one, carrying his head skewed over to the right and going up and down sort of sad. He stumbled, then caught himself, and came òn behind Mr. Ricky. He was white, what you might call an alkali white.

When Mr. Ricky stopped, the horse kept right on coming till he bunted Mr. Ricky between the shoulders with his nose. It was pink – like you get on a white rat. He stood sort of droopy, with a sway in his back to make a hammock look sick.

"That there horse," Jake said – "did he – did you buy him deliberate er did he jist happen to you?"

Mr. Ricky looked kind of hurt. "He ain't so much on the looks, but he's a horse a fella kin depend on – good an' quiet an' – "

"How old?"

"Dandy horse fer a kid to ride," said Mr. Ricky.

"How old?" asked Jake, looking at the horse's teeth.

" 'Bout ten," said Mr. Ricky.

Jake stepped back. "When a critter's that long o' the tooth, you don't count years – he's jist plumb aged."

"Where's the kid's maw?" said Mr. Ricky.

"Long ways fer a kid to climb up onto an' fall off of. Seventeen han's?"

"Sixteen two," said Mr. Ricky.

Jake spit. "Jist a Shetland. Course – that there sway in his back – bring a fella a lot closter to the groun'."

"I better see the kid's maw," said Mr. Ricky. "Where's the – "

"What you'd call a three-in-one horse," said Jake.

"Three-in-one!"

"Yep – wry neck, pop-eyes, jug-head – all in the same critter."

"You got no call to run down this here horse in front o' – "

"Ain't much, after a thoroughbred."

"Kid don't want no hot blood under him," snapped back Mr. Ricky. "Wants a quiet horse, jist like this here!" That will show you how much he knows what a kid wants under him! "I ain't wastin' any time talkin' with you when it's the kid's maw – "

Jake took the halter shank from Mr. Ricky. He walked the horse around, handed the rope back, then bent down and felt the front and hind legs. He had a puzzled look on his face when he straightened up again.

"Buttermilk's his name," Mr. Ricky said to me. "Got him from a fella useta call him Whisky, but he got stummick ulcers, so he changed his name to Buttermilk."

"The horse er the fella?" Jake said. He still looked like he was wondering about something.

"I ain't makin' no deal with you! It's the kid an' his – "

"Still can't figger her out," said Jake.

"Figure what out, Jake?" I said.

"Ain't string-halted, ner has he got the heaves. His shoulders don't slope so good, he's got him a couple a kidney sores, he's pigeon-toed. No splints, spavins, ringbone, ner bogs. I don't see how a horse with nothin' real bad wrong with him kin manage to look so goddam awful he – "

"You stop that sorta talk!" yelled Mr. Ricky. "He'll fatten into a real nice-lookin' – "

"You could fatten him from now till the ressy-rection," said Jake, "an' he'd still look bad enough to give a gopher the heartburn."

"All the same, Jake, he does look like a gentle horse." That was Ma who had come up.

"Gentle!" snorted Jake. "O' course he's gentle! If he wasn't he'd bust every bone in his goddam – "

"Please, Jake," Ma said, "watch your language in front of my son!" She turned to Mr. Ricky. "Perhaps you'd like to come to the house and – "

"Jist make sure the critter ain't got the sleepin' sickness," said Jake. He turned and headed for the barn, me after him.

"Jake," I said, "I hope she doesn't trade Fever – "

"Only one thing to do now," said Jake. "Go git Fever."

"What are we going to – "

"Git him; I'll bring the saddle out. You gotta show yer maw you kin ride him. If she could see you settin' on top of him, mebbe she wouldn't be so anxious to trade him off fer that there fox feed Ricky brung over. Git!"

When I came back with Fever, Jake threw the saddle on him. He turned to me.

"Git up!"

"Will he – do you think he'll buck, Jake?"

"Might," Jake said.

I rubbed the palms of my hands down the sides of my pants. "Does – it hurt to get throwed, Jake?"

"Sometimes." Jake looked at me. "Lots worse things than gittin' throwed."

"I don't feel so – "

"O' course you don't. Grab them lines shorter. Gimme yer foot."

I did.

"Ready?"

I jerked my head.

Jake's heave landed me in the saddle, and while I was feeling for the other stirrup with my foot, Fever jumped. Maybe he didn't jump so hard, but he threw me clear over the saddle horn. I slid right past his neck and hit the ground.

"Git up there!" Jake was looking down at me. "Git up on him agin – right now!"

"My knees, Jake – I couldn't grip him so good if he – Couldn't you sort of top him off for me – "

"Nope – wanta tell yer maw you bust him yerself, he was so gentle. Git up!"

I got.

This time I had both feet in the stirrups when Fever put his head down; there wasn't any horse past the saddle horn – just ground way down there. I lifted with Fever's hindquarters, and when he came down, the jolt made me slip sideways. When he started crow-hopping, that finished me. I lit right in the middle of the duckpond, and I felt my left elbow go numb. I'd hit it on a rock.

That was when I got mad – mad at Fever and at Jake, but maddest at myself.

I got into the saddle without Jake helping me. Fever stood. I took one end of the reins, and I gave him a dandy. His head went down; he sort of seized up under me. With both hands I grabbed that saddle horn, and with both legs I gripped as tight as I could. He wasn't shaking me loose!

Jake told me afterwards it looked just like corn popping, and me for the popcorn. I stuck him – for five bucks I stuck him, and then there weren't any more bucks left. The corner of the barn, the hogpens at the end of the corral, then the blacksmith shop and the stock trough were going past me dizzy as anything. I saw Jake running for the gate, and just as we came around he got it open.

Right through Ma's kitchen garden we went, through the caragana, the poplar windbreak, and out to the baldheaded prairie. Fever's head was lined out, and he was running! With his mane flying and his shoulders pounding, he was smoother than anything I ever sat on, smoother than a rocking-chair, smoother than cream pouring. I could hear the saddle creaking and my own blood hammering in my ears. The wind we made was at my mouth, filling my cheeks and blowing them out. I sat back, and it was just like waves washing and lifting me to the tune of his gallop.

I pulled at his head. I got it up and his gallop slowed. I leaned over and patted him on the neck; I talked to him.

And then he was down to a walk, a dancy walk, throwing his head up and dancing first to one side then to the other, his rump circling round.

All around us was the bald-headed prairie with the air soft and warm and the sky lifting up without a cloud in sight. A meadow lark sang to us. A badger ran funny over the prairie, with his hide swinging raggedly like a torn grey blanket.

As we headed back for the house, I saw a whirlwind come spinning over the summer fallow toward us. It hit us cool, a hot wind that turned cool against the sweat. It was cool for Fever, too, with his hide dark with sweat and the hair sort of thickened and half curling along his neck.

I leaned down and put my arms around his neck. I laid my face against it. I hugged him.

Jake was at the gate.

"I rode him, Jake!" I said. "I did it! He isn't mean – I rode him!"

Jake didn't say anything while he helped me down. He stood there with the reins in his hand, and he looked at me.

"What's wrong, Jake! What's the matt – "

"Yer maw," he said, "she went an' made a deal with Ricky – five dollars an' Buttermilk fer Fever."

I felt sick.

I guess I went around looking like I'd eaten horse-radish through a wove wire fence the next couple of days. Mr. Ricky had left Buttermilk; he was coming back the end of the week to get Fever. I didn't ride Fever. The way I felt, I didn't want to go near him, not when I knew that he wasn't my horse any more.

A couple of times I saw Ma looking at me kind of funny. I couldn't talk to her about it. The way I felt, I just as soon Fever died from the sleeping sickness that killed off five of Tincher's horses. I'd rather have him dead as somebody else own him, I figured, while I lay in bed the night before Mr. Ricky was to come and get him.

And then, while I lay there listening to Jake snore, I all of a sudden wanted to see Fever again. So I got up.

Inside the barn, I passed Baldy and Queen in their stalls. Fever wasn't in. I went out in the corral. The gate to the south pasture was open, and that was a funny thing; the bad slough's down there. Jake told me he'd thin my hide if I ever left that gate open. I headed back to the house.

Ma was standing at the stove the next morning. I sat down opposite Jake with his jaw going slow back and forth.

"Your pancakes, son."

"I'm not so hungry, Ma."

"Try and eat," she said. "You feel all right?"

I said I was all right.

"Your eyes – "

"Real windy yesterday," said Jake. "Mighta got some blow dirt into them." He got up. "Better go pump the stock trough full before – so's he kin have him a drink before – so's he kin have him a drink."

Ma was standing over me. "I'm sorry, son," she said. "I'm only trying to – You – you're pretty fond of Fever."

I didn't say anything. I couldn't.

"Buttermilk isn't a pretty horse, but he's – he's safe. It's hard to – when your father's away – till he gets back – I have to be both, son."

The diamonds on the oilcloth were all blurry.

"You went out last night."

I nodded my head. The diamonds were all spangled now.

"To see Fever?"

I jerked my head and a couple splashed on the table top.

Ma went to the stove. She didn't say anything for a long time. When I looked up I saw she had her back turned away. "All right," she said. She turned around with a real tight look on her face. "You win. You – Jake – Fever."

"Oh – Ma!"

"That's right. I won't let him go to Mr. Ricky. We'll keep him."

I'm real fussy about my ma.

Mr. Ricky was in the yard when we got out. Ma told him she'd changed her mind.

"Oh," Mr. Ricky said, and he jumped his Adam's apple. "I always like to think folks is as good as their word."

Ma's face flamed. "You can depend on my word, Mr. Ricky."

"We made us a deal," said Mr. Ricky. "That there five dollars I give you – I figger that cinched it. A deal's a deal."

"I'm asking you to release me," Ma said real quiet. "My son – "

"Nope," Mr. Ricky said.

I felt Ma's hand tighten on my shoulder.

"Perhaps you would be willing to take back the other horse and – and – twenty dollars for your – "

"Nope." Mr. Ricky turned to Jake. "Where's he at?"

"South pasture," Jake said. "Sooner you git him, the better. He's yore horse an' I don't like bein' responsible fer him no longer what I have to. Lotta sleepin' sickness around. Jist last week found him runnin' with some o' Tincher's horses. They lost five out of it, you know."

Mr. Ricky grunted.

"Say it's a bug gits in their ear," Jake said as we walked out in the south pasture, "goes to the brain. Ever see it?"

Mr. Ricky shook his head.

"Horrible," Jake said. "Not at first – jist dopey-lookin' – hide all rough – slabberin' at the mouth. I kin always tell by the hind legs."

We were passing the slough, real white, with alkali lying snowy along her rim.

" 'Tain't long till they're down, battin' their own brains

out," said Jake. "That's jist the way that Ed's done."

"Don't see that there horse," said Mr. Ricky.

We found him lying down in the brush.

"Takin' a lay-down in the shade," said Jake.

Fever started to get up; he lay back; he took another try at her; he stood.

"Say," said Mr. Ricky, "that horse don't look so good."

"He doesn't, Jake!"

"Looks dandy to me," said Jake.

On our way to the house, Mr. Ricky kept looking back at Fever. "He's slabberin'."

"Hot day," Jake said.

"His eyes is sorta sunk-lookin'." Mr. Ricky stopped. He watched Fever a minute. "Them hind legs – That horse is sick."

"He wasn't sick three days ago," said Jake, "when you made yer deal."

"He's sick," said Mr. Ricky again. "Jist a minnit!" Jake stopped.

"Hide rough – slabberin' at the mouth – eyes sunk – hin' legs – no wonder you was so anxious to git him off o' the place – said yerself he'd bin runnin' with Tincher's horses. You ain't foolin' me none – that there horse has got sleepin' sickness!"

"The hell he has!" Jake said.

"You ain't goin' to stick me with no – "

"A deal's a deal."

"Nothin's wrote down! Can't prove her! My word agin – "

"Ye're not gittin' out – "

"Tryin' to sell me a horse that'll be battin' out his brains before nightfall!"

Mr. Ricky started running for our yard, where he'd left Buttermilk tied up.

"Let him go," Jake said.

"But – Jake! What are we going to – what can we do for Fever!"

"Ain't nothin' a fella kin do fer sleepin' sickness," Jake said.

"Maybe we better shoot him before he gets to battin' his br – "

"You git to the house," Jake said. "Ast yer maw fer a quart bottle – fill her with raw linseed oil – "

"But – if you can't do anything for sleep – "

"Who said he had sleepin' sickness! Nothin' like a linseed-oil drench to bring a horse around after a touch o' alkali poisonin'. Show yuh not to leave gates open."

"But I didn't, Jake! I didn't leave the gate – "

"I didn't say you did! All I said was, 'Show you not to leave gates open.'" He looked down at me. " 'Cept once in a while."

I'm sort of fussy about Jake too.

10

Two Kinds of Sinner

EVER SINCE Ma quit cutting my hair for me, I go
in to Repeat Golightly's. He lets me sit right on the
chair; he doesn't put that board across any more. Most
of the time Jake, our hired man, takes me to town in the
democrat, and he was in the barbershop the afternoon Doc
Toovey got to talking how his paint horse, Spider, could
run the gizzard out of Auction Fever.

The afternoon the argument with Doc Toovey started,
Jake had got his shave and was sitting next to Old Man
Gatenby whilst Repeat cut my hair. I had my head tilted,
with my chin on my chest, and was looking up from under,
the way you do, when Repeat swung me around. Then I
could see myself over the tonic bottles and the clock with
its numbers all backward and Doc Toovey just in the doorway.

Doc runs the Crocus Hay and Feed and Livery. He is a
horse and cattle vet, and he has very white hair and a very

red face that is all the time smiling. His eyes will put you in mind of oat seeds, sort of.

"Anybody ahead of me?" he asked. His voice is kind of smily too.

"There's four shaves waitin'," Repeat said; "there's four fellas waitin' to git their shave."

"That's fine," Doc said, and he sat down in the chair between Old Man Gatenby and Jake. Jake slid over a little; he isn't so fussy about Doc Toovey; Doc would steal the well out of a person's yard when they weren't looking, Jake says. Jake has old-timer eyes that are squinty from looking into the sun an awful lot. He is pretty near always right.

Repeat went back to work on my hair. "She was smart," he said. "She was a smart little mare." He was talking about Dish Face, the black hackney he used to have in the early days.

"I knew a real smart horse once," Jake said. "Wasn't no hot blood neither – just an ordinary work horse. He run for Parliament on the Lib'ral ticket."

Doc stopped with a plug of tobacco halfway to his mouth. "That's plum foolish." He bit a corner off.

"The heck it is," said Jake. "He was a real bright horse, an' when he seen all the combines an' tractors comin' West he – what else was there fer him to do but go into politics?"

"Well – " Doc leaned sideways in his chair and spit into the spittoon. "I ain't interested in smart horses. But you take running horses, like my paint. He can run."

" 'Bout as fast as a one-arm fella on a handcar," said Jake.

Doc Toovey smiled at Jake. "Ain't nothing around here can beat him."

"That right?" said Jake.

"The kid here has got a nice-looking horse," said Repeat. "I say this here kid's horse is a nice look – "

"I've seen him," said Doc. "He ain't no match for Spider." He smiled at me.

"He can nail Spider's hide to a fence post," I said. "Recess time out at Rabbit Hill he – "

"You wasn't int'rested in findin' out, was you?" Jake asked Doc real polite.

"Might be." Doc spit again. "Might even put a little bet on it."

"How much?" Jake asked him.

"Whatever you want."

"Fifty dollars," said Jake, "and Repeat holds the money."

"I'll hold her," said Repeat, letting me down out of the chair. "You fellas can give her to me and I'll hold her fer you."

"Fine," said Doc. Both him and Jake reached into their pockets.

They worked it out we were going to hold the race next Saturday along the C.P.R. tracks behind Hig Wheeler's lumberyards. When they were done Doc climbed into the barber chair.

"You ain't next," said Repeat. "I say you ain't the – "

"That's all right," said Doc. "Those others ain't in a hurry."

"I'm in a hell of a hurry," said Old Man Gatenby.

"I don't really need a four-bit haircut, Repeat." Doc smiled up at him. "Just give her a sort of a neck trim. Fifteen cents."

Going out home I sat with Jake in the democrat, watching Baldy's hindquarters tipping first one side then the other, real regular but sort of jerky, like Miss Henchbaw when she leads the singing at Rabbit Hill with her stick. Jake didn't say anything for a long way. By the road a meadow lark spilled some notes off of a strawstack. A jack rabbit next the bar pit undid himself for a few hops then sat startled, with his black-tipped ears straight up.

Jake spit curvy into the breeze. "I wouldn't say nothin' to yer maw."

"About Fever racin' Doc's paint, Spider?"

"Yep."

The rabbit went bouncing to beat anything over the baldheaded prairie. Over to the right of the road a goshawk came sliding down real quiet, slipping his black shadow over the stubble.

"Way yer maw looks at it, bettin' ain't right. I guess next to eatin' tobacco, yer maw hates gamblin'. I wouldn't say nothin' to her – ain't like you was doing the bettin'. All you're doin' is racing." Jake turned to me. "Like she's always sayin', 'Gents don't bet, an' gents don't chaw.'" He spit, and slapped the reins. "Git yer nose out of it, Baldy."

Jake turned to me again. "Fever's gonna run that there long-geared Spider right into the ground!"

All that week I raced Fever – at recess – after four; and like he always does, he beat everything at Rabbit Hill. At home Jake worked on him till he started dandy nine times out of ten. When he finished the distance he wasn't blowing hardly at all, and stepped away all dancy, like he was walking on eggs.

"He'll do," Jake said.

Then Ma found out. She came out to the shed whilst I was washing up for supper.

"I was talking with Mrs. Fotheringham today, son." She waited like she wanted me to say something. I pretended I was getting soap out of my ears. "On the phone," Ma said.

I poured out the basin into the slop pail.

"Mrs. Fotheringham was talking to Doctor Fotheringham. He was talking with Mr. Golightly. She told me there was to be a race Saturday."

"Did she?" I said.

"Yes." Ma's dark eyes were looking right at me. "Between Fever and Dr. Toovey's horse."

I could feel my face getting burny.

"There is some money involved. Fifty dollars. Is that right?"

I jerked my head.

"Why did you do it, son?"

I didn't get any answer out.

"You knew I wouldn't approve. You know what I think of that sort of thing. You know it's wrong, don't you?"

I said, yes, I guessed I did.

"I blame you just as much as I do Jake. I'm beginning to think Auction Fever's not good for you."

"Oh yes he is, Ma!"

"Not if he's going to get you mixed up in – in – *gambling*."

I looked down at my boots.

"I honestly think I'd just as soon see you chewing tobacco, son!" Ma turned away. At the kitchen door she swung around again. "There's not to be a race Saturday or any day. Not with Doctor Toovey's horse or any horse!"

She gave it to Jake too. She told him to call the race off because it was immoral. That means bad. Jake kicked, but it didn't do him any good.

We found Doc Toovey leaning against his livery stable. His tobacco cud had bulged out the side of his face, so his smile was sort of lopsided. "All set to get beat in that race?" he called.

"Ain't gonna be no race," Jake said.

"Huh!"

"Kid's maw won't let him."

"Well – " Doc smiled down to me – "that's just too bad."

"It is," Jake said.

" 'Course, you'd have lost your 50 dollars anyway."

"Huh!"

"This way you don't prolong the agony."

"What you mean?"

"You called off the race," said Doc. "I didn't. Don't expect to get your money back, do you?"

"I shore as hell do!"

Doc spit, and a little puff of dust came up. "Well, you ain't getting it."

Jake looked at Doc all smily; he looked at the manure fork leaning against the stable-wall; he looked back at Doc Toovey again. Real quiet, he said, "You'd look awful funny with that there stickin' outa yer wishbone, Doc."

"Would I?" Doc kept right on smiling.

Later when Jake told Repeat Golightly, Repeat said:

"Ain't much you can do, Jake. I say if he don't want to leave you have the money there ain't much you can – "

Jake slammed out of the barbershop, me right behind.

Ma didn't give an inch. She's sure set against betting – and chewing tobacco.

The next time we were in to Crocus we met Doc Toovey in front of the Royal Bank.

"Got a new critter today, Jake," he said. "Bent Golly sold him to me. Figgered you might like to race the kid's buckskin against him."

Jake pushed on past.

"I'd have to get odds," Doc called after us. "He's a mule!"

The next time was in Snelgrove's bakery, when Doc saw me and Jake through the window, eating ice cream. He came in and he said he had a jack rabbit he wanted to put up against Fever. A week later he asked Jake if he thought Fever might give a prairie chicken a good run. Jake mumbled something under his breath.

" 'Course you might be scared, same as you were the time before, and want to back out of it," Doc said. "If you haven't got the guts – "

"Guts!" Jake yelled. "We got 'em all right! We'll show you! That there race is on again! Same place, same distance, and double the bet, you scroungin', stubble-jumpin', smily-faced son of a hardtail!"

Afterward I said to Jake:

"What'll Ma – "

"We're racin'," Jake said.

"But, Ma won't – "

"Yer maw figgers 'tain't right, but what that there – what that – what he's doin' to us is plum immortal too, an' if I got to take my pick between two kinds of a sinner, I know which kind I'm takin'!"

And that was how come we ended up behind Hig Wheeler's the next Saturday, all set to race Fever and the paint. Jake and me brought Fever in behind the democrat. At the last moment Ma decided to come with us. Jake told her we were getting Fever's hind shoes fixed.

We left Ma at Mrs. Fotheringham's, then we headed for the race.

Half the folks from Crocus were there, and nearly everyone from Rabbit Hill district. Jake and Doc Toovey weren't the only ones betting.

Mr. MacTaggart, that is mayor of Crocus, he was the starter and he sent Johnny Totcoal down to the Western Grain Elevator, where we had to make the turn. That turn had bothered Jake a lot when we were working out Fever. Spider was a cow horse and could turn on a dime. "He's got you there," Jake had said to me, "but I got a little trick to even that up." Then he'd showed me how to grab the horn with both hands and up into the saddle without touching a foot to the stirrup. Doc hadn't kicked when Jake told him the race ought to be from a standing start beside the horses. I guess he figured a small kid couldn't get up as fast as he could with his longer legs.

"Now, fellas," Mr. MacTaggart was saying, "you start from here, each one beside his horse. When I say 'go,' into the saddle and down to the stake by the Western Grain Elevator, then around an' back."

Doc nodded and smiled; he had a chew of tobacco the size of a turkey hen's egg. Looking at the paint horse I felt sort of grasshoppery to my stomach; my knees weren't so good either. Doc's Spider was long in the leg, and he looked like he could line out if he wanted to.

"Real pretty." Doc had his hand on Fever's neck, stroking his gold hide and running his fingers through his silver mane. "But that don't make 'em run any faster."

If being ugly made a horse fast, I was thinking that jug head of Doc's must be a whirlwind!

"How old is he?" Doc was up at Fever's head now.

"Two and a half."

Doc lifted Fever's lip and looked inside.

"Let that there horse alone!" Jake had left Mr. Mac-Taggart and come up.

"Just looking at his teeth," said Doc.

"Only ones he's got," said Jake. "Keep yer han's off that horse!"

"Ready, fellas?" Mr. MacTaggart called.

Doc jumped back beside Spider. I put both hands on top of the saddle horn.

"GO!"

I into that saddle like a toad off a hot stove, and I dug my heels into Fever and gave him the leather both sides. He jumped straight into a gallop. Looking back I saw Doc's leg just coming down over the saddle.

Fever had his head up and was fighting like anything. "Come on, Fever!" I yelled at him. His head came down again and he threw his shoulders into it. Then Spider and Doc were beside us, and Fever had his head up again. Doc passed us, and Fever wasn't running at all! He was trying, but I'd seen old Baldy do better.

"Please, Fever – *please!*" I leaned down over his neck. "Come on, boy!" He threw back his head, and I felt something wet on my cheek – foam blowing back.

Spider reached the stake five lengths ahead of us. He made the turn like you snap your fingers. We were halfway down the second lap when the paint went across the finish line. Doc was over by Repeat Golightly when I climbed down from Fever.

Poor Fever's sides were heaving, and he was still tossing his head, and me, I wished I wasn't a human being at all.

"He didn't run, Jake! He didn't run a bit."

"Some horses are like that," said Doc. He watched Jake feeling Fever's front legs. "When they get up against something good they quit."

"This horse ain't no quitter!" Jake had straightened up. "There's somethin' fishy about this – "

"Jake!" That was Ma, with her face all red and her eyes brighter than anything. Jake saw Ma and he swallowed and kind of ducked. She grabbed me by the arm, hard. "You've deliberately disobeyed me, son! You've – Jake!"

Jake had hold of Fever's nose and was sticking his finger in it. "I'm lookin' fer somethin'," Jake said. "Somebody went an' – "

"I forbade you to race that horse and you went ahead, against my wishes! I – it – " Ma had got so tangled up in her britching she couldn't talk.

"Mebbe a sponge," Jake said. "Cuts off their wind."

"Ma, Auction Fever he didn't run at – "

"That's enough!" Ma yanked on my arm. "I know now that I can't – " She stared at me, and it was like her face froze over all of a sudden.

"What have you got in your mouth?"

I didn't have anything in my mouth.

She jerked around to Jake. "The most despicable thing I've ever seen!"

"They claim water in their ear – "

"Teaching my son to chew tobacco!"

"Chew tobacco!" Jake's mouth dropped open and his eyes bugged.

Ma stepped forward and she stuck out her finger. It came away from the corner of my mouth, all brown. "There!"

"Now jist a minnit," said Jake. "Take it easy."

"Betting is bad enough – but – chewing – "

"Don't give him that money!" Jake's face was all lit up like he'd eaten a sunset. Repeat looked over at him, with the money he'd been going to give Doc still in his hand.

Jake walked across to Fever. He pulled out Fever's underlip. He looked, then he lifted the lip, grunted, and stuck his crooked finger in. It came out with the biggest jag of chewing tobacco I ever saw.

"Well, now," Jake said as he walked toward Doc, "ain't that interestin'? Horse that's fussy about chewin' tobacco. Wouldn't be Black Stag like you had in your mouth before the race – before you took a look at Fever's teeth?"

"I don't know what you're talking about." Doc was smiling, but it was a pretty sick-looking smile.

"The hell you don't!"

"Doctor Toovey!" That was Ma, and the way she was looking at Doc you could easy tell she used to be a school-teacher. "Did you or did you not put a – a – cud of chewing tobacco in my – in that horse's mouth?"

I knew how Doc felt – like when the whole room gets quiet and Miss Henchbaw is looking right at you and you know you're in for it.

"Makes 'em slobber," said Jake. "Then they swallow it down an' it cuts their wind."

"Will the horse be all right, Jake?" Ma asked.

"Shore," said Jake. "Won't hurt him none. 'Fact he's all right now."

Ma's face sort of tightened. She whirled back to Doc. "You are going to race! You will climb up on that horse and run an honest race against my son! Don't interrupt, Doctor Toovey."

"I ain't – that kid don't weigh more'n a grasshopper – "

"He hasn't put on any weight since you first arranged the race," Ma snapped.

Doc looked at Jake and the other folks around him; folks from our section aren't so fussy about seeing a kid and his horse get diddled.

You should of felt Fever under me that second race! He ran smooth, with his silver mane flying and his neck laid out. He ran like the wind over the edge of the prairie coming to tell everybody they can't live forever – slick as the wind through a field of wheat – slicker than peeled saskatoons. He's the only horse living, Jake says, with three gears in high. He's the only horse can make my throat plug up that way and my chest nearly bust.

Doc Toovey ought to have known better. My Fever is a Gent. And Gents don't chaw!

11

The Day Jake Made Her Rain

I COULD feel both of my legs getting kind of numb the way they do when you are sitting on the edge of something a long time. But Jake and Old Man Gatenby didn't let on they were getting numb. They were too mad.

Jake was sitting beside me on our horse trough and he had his long legs kinked up at the knees just like a grasshopper ready to spring. "You take Hatfield," he said.

"You take him," Old Man Gatenby said real snappy. Old Man Gatenby and Jake are both old, but Old Gate's face has taken it worse than Jake's – enough wrinkles to hold a three-day rain.

Even under the grey stubble you could tell from Jake's face that he was mad. It was red and had knotty sort of bulges at the corners of his jaw. His Adam's apple was jumping too. Like he was trying to get a hold of himself he kept quiet a minute whilst he stared at a Wine-dot pecking in the dust; his eyes that are that faded sort of blue, stared at Old Man Gatenby's dog lying with his long tongue spilled out and panting.

There hadn't been any rain the last three weeks of July and even the hen looked thirsty.

"He brung rain to Medicine Hat," Jake said. "Then there was that other fella – come through Crocus districk with alla his machinery set up on a C.P.R. flatcar. He – "

"Jist a sprinkly little shower didn't even lay the dust," said Old Man Gatenby.

Jake shifted to get himself easier on the edge of the trough. He squinted up at some fat popcorn clouds over top of us; he kept right on looking at that hot blue sky that had forgot how to rain. "He contracted to git paid fer any rain he brung over an' above the average rainfall."

"Didn't do so good out Yalla Grass way," said Old Gate. "Ner at Brokenshell – ner Union Jack – they run him outa Broomhead."

"Nothin' to do with him rainin'," interrupted Jake.

"It shore as – "

"That was accounta the poker game over the China-man's – "

"Was not!"

"She was!" Jake looked right into Gate's eyes the way they were like cloves stuck into a little round apple – one you let lay around a long time till it got all puckered and shrivelly.

Old Man Gatenby pulled out a plug and squeezed off a corner with his knife. Then he lifted her to his mouth. "No rain maker," he said with his voice stubborn and slow and like it hurt him to keep it down the way he was doing, "with no rain machine never brought no rain to nobody!" Then he spit.

"Don't!" Jake yelled and Gate nearly fell into the trough.

"Huh!"

"Don't spit!"

Old Man Gatenby gawped at Jake.

"It's sinful," Jake said.

"Sinful!"

"Wastin' yer moisture that way."

Old Gate looked at Jake like he was a fork going into a thrashing machine. "Tryin' to change the subjeck when yer sooperstishus – "

" 'Tain't sooperstishus," Jake said. "If they got the right kinda machine, then they kin do it."

"They kin do it in a pig's ear," said Gate.

"A heck of an awkward place to raise wheat."

"They kin not – "

"They kin so! I seen it done!" yelled Jake.

"You ain't." I was thinking it's funny how when old folk get to arguing they do it a lot like the kids do at recess at Rabbit Hill.

"I done it myself!" Jake was bellering.

"You did n – !" Old Man Gatenby's mouth snapped shut. His little eyes sparkled at Jake. "You whut!"

Jake swallowed quick. "Why – I – afore I come to Crocus districk."

"You bet it was afore you come here," agreed Gate. "Where the heck did you do any rainin'?"

"In o' four – Manyberries way."

"Is that so?" Old Gate's voice was real polite.

"Yep," said Jake. "Use to call me Sheet-lightnin' Trumper."

"Did they now? You have much of a success of this here rain makin'?"

"In a way I did," Jake said. "Then in a way I didn't."

"Either you brung her down er you didn't bring 'er down," said Old Gate.

"I brung her down all right," said Jake. "Trouble was I didn't have no control when I rained. Lotsa power – no control – none a them light misty rains – them skimpy quick little summer showers – when I rained I really rained."

"That's nice," said Old Man Gatenby and the way he said it you knew he didn't think it was nice at all.

"Take Dominion Day in o' five – got her turned on an' couldn't git her turned off all through August an' September. Har'ly nobody got thrashed at all so she had to stan' in the stook right through till spring – then they didn't git no crop."

"Why not?"

"Mice," said Jake. "Stooks was fulla mice. Go by a field an' see alla them spikers an' field pitchers working without no pants – "

"Without any pants, Jake!" I said.

"Yep. Stick a fork into a stook an' out run the mice an' up a fella's pant leg. Had to thrash without no pants. Mice et alla the wheat – jist straw left. Can't thrash straw."

"To git back to this here rain makin'," Old Gate said nasty. "How did – "

"Never got away from her," said Jake. "Jist explainin' how come folks wasn't so fussy about me rainin'! Too much moisture. Then, too, she was sort of a onhealthy rain – onnatural – folks got all kindsa stuff outa it – colds – flu – that's when my rheumatism started up the first time."

"I'd settle fer double pneumonia to git some moisture on that flax a mine," said Gate. Old Man Gatenby had two hundred acres of flax – flax is just as thirsty as wheat or rye or oats. "An' the way this here droughty weather has bin, makes a fella real disgusted to hear you blowin' about how you kin rain an' what all rain makers kin do with their machines – 'nough to give a gopher the heartburn." He went to spit, then changed his mind. "Sacerlidge."

"You don't believe me," said Jake.

"You bet I don't! Er else you'd rig up yer rain machine an' rain."

"I told you why I quit."

"You ain't told noth' cept a whoppin' jag a lies – Sheet-lightnin' Trumper."

Jake's Adam's apple was going up and down like a bucket in a well. "Ef I wanted to rain," he said, "why I could do her right now."

"I'm callin' you," Old Gate said and his little eyes looked at Jake real cold. "Bring on yer rain machine."

"I ain't got her made."

"Well, make her."

"I ain't – the – 'tain't all that easy to – "

"See what I mean – just like I said – a whoppin' jag a – "

"Don't say it," Jake warned him, "er you won't never see rain again!" He got off of the horse trough. "I'll rain," he said.

"When?" said Gate.

"Soon as I git my machine put together."

"When'll that be?"

"When I'm ready." Jake spit.

"Don't!" Old Man Gatenby yelled and Jake just looked at him.

"Come on, Kid," he said, "we got chores to do."

Jake was quiet all through supper and Ma looked at him like she wondered what was the matter. She said: "I guess this dry weather is getting on everyone's nerves."

Jake went right on with his saskatoon pie, eating it real careful with his knife and fork. Jake is a neat eater.

"Jake's going to make a rain machine," I said.

There was a clatter and Jake was looking up from a purple stain over the oilcloth. Ma's eyes were wide and dark on Jake.

"If a person would keep his mouth shut," Jake said, "he wouldn't get him into so much trouble." He got up jerky from the table and he started for the door. He turned back. "Not that he won't have him a crop a trouble anyways, but maybe she won't go so many bushels to the acre. An' maybe, if he keeps his mouth shut, she won't grade so high when he gits her. Number one hard." He turned to the door, then back again. "Don't fergit that, Kid." As he went out he said, "Like I done this afternoon."

I didn't dare ask Jake what he was going to work on when he got out paper and a stubby pencil that night before bedtime. He bent over the table with his shadow all sprawly over the kitchen wall and flickering from the lamp light. I pretended like I was reading *The Prairie Farm Review* and all about folks with critters that are sick with something and how to can vegetables. You could hear the cream separator purring out in the back shed where Ma was and the moths ticking against the lamp chimney.

Jake grunted and threw down the pencil. "Yer bedtime, ain't it, Kid?"

All the next day, whilst we were haying, Jake was quiet and he would say yes or he would say no or he would grunt at you. That was all. I was kind of glad to leave him and the rack and go down to the road for the mail. When I got a look at the *Crocus Breeze* that Mr. Cardwell had left in our box, I ran for Jake. He was really in trouble.

When Jake saw it, he just stood there with his fork in his hand and he looked kind of sick. "It's Gate," he said. "He done it."

"What are you going to do, Jake!"

Jake shook his head slow and his eyes were looking off over our crop turning brown along the edges for want of moisture. He rubbed his chin and it made a scrapy sound. He looked up at the sky, then off to the horizon. Way off there you could see a speck.

"Only one thing to do, Kid," he said.

"What?"

"Make me a machine."

"But – "

"This here," Jake slapped at the paper, "this here about

me bein' a rain maker an' about me makin' a machine – it – Kid, I guess there's worse things than havin' folks laff at you, but I don't know what they are."

The speck off in the sky wasn't a hawk; you could hear it now. Jimmy Shoelack. Jimmy was in the Air Force and he farms for Mrs. Christiansen who went back to the Old Country. He has a little yellow plane he uses for crop dusting and taking fellows out hunting antelope and folks up for rides at fairs around our district. That's the only thing Jake and Old Man Gatenby agree about – hating Jimmy Shoelack's airplane the way it buzzes all over like an angry wasp, scaring teams and stock.

But Jake wasn't paying any attention when Jimmy's plane came over us low. He said:

"I'm knocking off for the rest of the afternoon, Kid. Gotta git busy with some inventin'."

Three days later Old Man Gatenby showed up at our place to borrow our post-hole auger – at least that was what he said. Jake was real polite to him, just like he didn't get them to print that story about Jake in the *Crocus Breeze*. After Jake had got him the auger, he said:

" 'Bout that there machine. Lotta folks been askin' me when she'll be ready. August Petersen figgers his crop's only good fer another week, an' – "

"I'm workin' on her," Jake said. "I'm workin' on her."

"Well," said Old Gate, "it would be kinda nice to see somethin'."

Without saying anything Jake turned away and started walking toward the chophouse, me and Old Man Gatenby following after. Jake threw open the door and he stepped aside.

Old Man Gatenby's face, with his chin nearly touching his nose, poked out like a rooster getting ready to fight. He peered into the chophouse. "What's that!"

"A rain machine," said Jake.

I looked in. I saw sort of a cross between a wind electric and a gas motor and two lightning rods. I looked again. There were two blue bulbs.

"Call that a rain machine!" said Old Gate.

"She shore is," said Jake. "Ain't got her perfected yet."

"Turn her on," said Gate. "Let's see her run."

"Can't."

"Why not?"

"She's set for hail."

"Well then – onset her."

"That's what ain't perfected," Jake said. "She's all ready to go except fer that one little bug in her. I ain't bringin' no hail down on – "

"Say," said Old Man Gatenby, "ain't them blue bulbs sort of familiar?"

Jake almost caught Gate's nose in the door when he slammed it shut. "That there's the machine I used bufore. She worked then. She'll work agin. She was shore dry them days – had this skinned a mile. Dry! Not a slough in the districk, jist dust. Seen the frogs settin' up to their eyes in dust, jist their two bump eyes showin'.'"

"Them blue bulbs – " started Gate.

"All over the prairie where the sloughs use to be, little puffs a dust where the frogs was jumpin'. You'd see a frog jump, there'd be a plop a dust, then you'd see him swimmin' the way a frog does – underdust swimmin' – not quite so clear as underwater swimmin'. Hearin' 'em croakin' in their dust spring nights was kinda nice, made a fella remember she was spring at first – "

"At first, Jake, what – "

"After a couple of dry years, them winds lickin' up the top soil an' pilin' it against the fences an' houses an' granaries, wasn't no dust left in them sloughs no more." Jake stared at the ground and he said real sad, "Come the next spring not a frog in a slough, kinda tragical the way they died, lacka dust."

Old Man Gatenby had his face screwed up sour. "When," he said, "do you intend on rainin'?"

Jake cocked his head and he pursed his mouth. "End a this week, the beginnin' a the next."

"That's all I wanted to know," said Gate.

"More likely beginnin' a the next," said Jake, and I heard him muttering something about change of the moon.

Now Jake didn't seem so happy about his rain machine; he didn't act so perky about it as he had when he was showing it to Old Man Gatenby. He tinkered with it a bit, but most of the time whilst we finished up the haying, he was looking up into the sky. When you felt that wind oven-hot against your cheek, and when you tasted the dust dry in your throat, it was kind of hard to believe what Jake said about rain machines.

Wednesday our well went dry.

Thursday the *Crocus Breeze* announced Reverend Cameron was going to have a praying-for-rain Sunday. There was a little piece saying that Jake Trumper was going to rain on Tuesday next at Tincher's back forty where the ground rose between the correction line and Government Road. "He picks my day an' he picks my place," was all Jake said.

Friday Queen and Duke bolted so Jake fell off a load of hay and lit on his head. Here was how it happened.

We had a big load on and I had a hold of the lines and Jake was crawling to me when Jimmy Shoelack's plane came low and fast as a scalded coyote over the rise of the draw. He headed straight for the team. Duke reared up in his harness, then Queen; then they both began to run. It took me the whole field and the load of hay to get them stopped. I turned to Jake, only he wasn't on the load any more.

I tied them to the fence, then I ran back to where we'd been loading.

With his feet straight out in front of him, Jake was sitting on the bald-headed prairie right where he'd landed.

He wasn't cussing. He was just sitting there and looking off into the distance.

"You all right, Jake?"

He just went right on sitting there and looking kind of stupid.

"You all right, Jake!"

He was getting up slow and creaky, breathing hard the way you do after you've run a long ways. He started off walking.

"This way, Jake," I said.

He didn't even hear me. Just like he was dreaming he kept on walking in the opposite direction from our house. I ran to catch up. "You better come home, Jake. Take a lay-down till you feel bett – "

He shook me off.

"That's the wrong way, Jake."

"Wanta use Tincher's phone."

"I'll go phone Dr. Fotheringham," I said.

"Wanta use Tincher's phone. Wanta git Jimmy Shoelack bad."

"Jake," I said, "just report him. They'll fix him for what he did – "

"Wanta use Tincher's phone. Wanta thank him."

"Thank – Jake!" I yelled, "you come on home with me on the rack!"

Jake kept right on walking.

He got back late, whilst Ma was cleaning up the supper dishes. He went out to milking, singing "The Letter Edged In Black"; he came back with the milk pails, singing "The Baggage Coach Ahead".

He didn't go to church with Ma and me on Sunday, said he had to go over and see Jimmy Shoelack. The Reverend Cameron prayed for rain; he said for everybody to go right on praying next week and he'd take another try at her the following Sunday.

Monday a big parcel came for Jake in the mail.

"Is that for the rain machine?" I asked him.

"You might say she was, Kid."

"You worried, Jake – about tomorrow?"

He looked up at the sky.

"Do you really think she'll make rain?"

" 'Tain't a rain *makin'* machine," Jake said sharp.

"But you told Old Gate – "

"She's a rain machine. Ain't no machine kin *make* rain – that's plumb silly – jist bring her down if she's up there."

"I see," I said. "Jake."

"Yeah?"

"Those there blue bulbs Old Man Gatenby said – "

"Don't pay no attention to what he says."

"But, they look a lot like your – "

"Kid," Jake said, "when you say yer 'Now I Lay Me Down' tonight, after that there part about blessin' folks, stick in about sendin' a bunch of grey cloud tomorrah."

I promised I would.

The Lord must of heard. The next day, whilst Jake put up his rain machine on a platform in Tincher's corner, the grey clouds built up. By afternoon she was dark clear to the horizon, but that didn't mean anything; she'd done that lots of times without raining.

Everybody from our district came. They brought their lunches; they sat in the shade of their cars or their rigs and ate and drank coffee out of thermos jugs. Mr. Tincher organized some kids' races just like a Sunday-school picnic at Ashton's grove. Stevie Kiziw and me came first in the potato sack race; Axel Rasmussen was first in the egg and spoon race. Jimmy Shoelack was taking folks up for a cent a pound.

About four o'clock Jake got up on his platform. He

looked down at the folks all gathered around and some kids playing tag at one end of the platform. He looked up at the sky thick with soft grey like a goose.

"Now look," he said, "this here is a rain machine. I made it." He stopped like he was looking for words. "I aim to rain with it. I – ain't gonna explain the principle she works on – rain makin's a lot like other things, she takes faith. I'd say rain makin' was about one per cent machine an' ninety-nine per cent faith."

"Fergit the hot air an' git on to the rain!" yelled Mr. Botton.

" 'Tain't more wind we want!" That was Old Man Gatenby.

"All right," Jake said back at them. "But she won't work without faith, no more'n what she'll work without gas. I gotta have yer faith – all the faith in this here districk. Its gotta grow outa you folks wantin' the rain I'm gonna bring. You gotta wanta smell her cool on the air, an' wanta hear her slappin' loud on the roof, fillin' up them thirsty cracks in yer land, sloppin' outa yer stock troughs, fillin' an' risin' in yer sloughs an' wells!

"I gotta have faith from the women folk, too. You gotta want me to rain as bad as you want pansies lookin' up at you from yer flower beds, as bad as sweet peas an' hollyhocks is thirsty fer something besides soapy throw-out water, as bad as you wanta write down stuff outa the Hudson's Bay catalogue for yer kids!"

Jake's grey hair was standing right up on end, kind of misty. He seemed to be looking through the crowd for something. I turned around and I saw Jimmy Shoelack slipping away.

Jake said, "You gotta have faith she's gonna happen! You gotta know it in yer gizzard an' yer heart an' yer soul! You gotta know her – if I was you I'd take an' put something over my head, Mrs. Totcoal!" Mrs. Johnny Totcoal reached back and came up with a quilt from the democrat for her head and shoulders. "You gotta know her!" Jake was yelling, "clear as spring water!

"Any of you folks has snuffy teams get a good holt on them lines!" I saw Mr. Sawyer reaching forward for the reins. "I want yer faith – an' I'm a gonna git it!"

He, had it. You could tell. I'm only a kid, but I could smell faith all over the place. You could see it in folks' eyes. They knew Jake was going to rain; they knew it because it was ten times easier to know he would than it was to know he wouldn't.

"Stan' well back, folks!" Jake was yelling, "an' gimme room! Git a holt of yer kids fer I aim tuh rain!"

He gave the flywheel of the rain machine a spin; she coughed, she missed, she coughed again. Then she was going full blast. Jake struck a match on the seat of his overalls. *Whooooshshshs*, like a long breath between your teeth – and another and another and another – four rockets were trailing their fire tails into the sky.

Long and lean and angly Jake was facing the crowd again. You could hear his voice high and thin above the machine and something else. Then I realized it was the sound of Jimmy Shoelack's plane taking off. You could smell gas sharp on the air and you could see sparks wriggling and twisting between the two blue bulbs on the rain machine. Looking at those lightning rods pointing straight up to the sky and that motor chugging along, you could almost feel the machine hauling and drawing and pulling at that moisture up in those grey clouds – just like sucking pop through a straw and out of a bottle.

Something was wrong. The machine had stopped, and Jake was looking off to where the sound of Jimmy Shoelack's plane was fading away. He said real quiet:

"That's her, folks."

You could hear them breathing loud all around you. Old Man Gatenby coughed. The Botton kid let a holler out

of him. There was the tinkle of halter shanks, the creak of
harness. A car horn honked loud from somebody moving
quick and hitting it with their elbow. Mrs. Totcoal took the
quilt off of her head. Everybody was turning their eyes
away like they were embarrassed.

I looked up to the platform where Jake was still standing. Just a dead machine – a gas motor, two lightning rods,
the blue bulbs off of a rheumatism machine and our hired
man.

There was no faith in the faces of folks hooking up their
traces and turning to their cars and taking a hold of their
kids by the hands and not saying anything.

She sort of burst; she didn't take a few minutes for you
to realize what was happening; she didn't start off with a
few drops spanking you on the head or the cheek or the
back of your hand; she up and let go all of a sudden. Folks
quit whatever they were doing and they stood with their
lower lips over their upper ones like it was something to
taste and eat; the hides on all the horses were all of a sudden
dark and gleamy; the shoulders on Jake's coat were soaked
in no time and the drops running crooked white tracks down
through the dust over his face; the women's dresses were
plastered to them like your cotton bathing suit after a swim.
She was sure rainin'!

Johnny Totcoal let a whoop and he off with his coat and
he ripped open his shirt without doing the buttons and
stood with the rain streaming through the hair on his chest.
Up went the Reverend Cameron's long arms and he
shouted, "The Lord be praised!"

Old Man Gatenby's mouth came shut like a gopher trap.
"The Lord nothin'!" he yelled. "Sheet-lightnin' Trumper!"

Jake just stood there in his rain.

It was after we got home I said:

"Jake, why did Jimmy Shoelack – "

"Like everythin' else," Jake said, "there's bin a lotta advancement in rain makin'! That day Jimmy's plane sent me kitin' off of the hay, kinda reminded me of a article I read in the *Prairie Farm Review*." He looked down at me for a minute. "Ever hear tell a dry ice, Kid?"

I looked right back at him. "Sure," I said, "it was all over the prairies the year of the blue snow. That was when the dust all froze into solid cakes."

Jake looked at me kind of funny. He started to say something, but he changed his mind.

He knows better than to try fooling me.

12

The Princess and the Wild Ones

WHEN Miss Henchbaw got up and stood there with her hands folded across her stomach, she had her mouth sort of turned up at the corners, like when she's got something to tell us and it's good. I was looking clear across the room at Lazarus Lefthand. He's in the Grade Ones. We only got four of them. Lazarus' hair is very black and it puts you in mind of those chrysanthemums. He is the only Indian kid we got in Rabbit Hill School.

Miss Henchbaw she looked down at us; her grey hair, that's piled up like those round loaves of bread, was under the writing on the board:

> THE GIRL PLAYS WITH THE DOG.
> IT IS FUN TO PLAY.

"Children!" Her voice all the time goes up at the end. "There will be a half holiday. Mr. MacTaggart has spoken to the school board and we've decided – they think it would be nice if the girls could wear white dresses with red and blue sashes. The school board are supplying the flags. They'd like the Grade Five choir to open with 'O Canada'." She stared at Stevie Kiziw twirling his ruler on his compass. "Steve!"

Steve's ruler clattered on the desk.

"Now – just the first verse. And Mr. MacTaggart says that whether or not the Princess gets off the train – if she only steps out onto the – "

"Caboose," Stevie said.

"Observation car – he would like a presentation of flowers by one of the school children."

The kids didn't make much noise; you could just hear them sort of draw in their breath. Mariel Abercrombie stuck up her hand. She has chops. "Mother still has dahlias and asters and marigolds and golden glow, Miss Hench-baw."

"That's nice, Mariel . . ."

"They're the last but they're nice still and there's enough of them for a bouquet and nobody else in town have their flowers last as long as ours – or come out so soon."

"Then we can depend on Mariel's mother for flowers to hand to the Princess . . ."

"Who's going to hand them up to her?" That was LaPrelle Rasmussen.

"Oh – Mother – if they were our flowers I think Mother would expect *me* to hand them to the Princess . . ." faltered Mariel.

"It's quite an honour to have your flowers *given*, Mariel. I think for the next few weeks we'll keep a close record – attendance – standing in arithmetic and writing and reading. The one who has the highest average – I think as a reward that child would be the proper one to hand the bouquet to the Princess on the station platform."

When I got home after four, Jake was pumping water into the stock trough. Jake's our hired man that helps Ma and me farm our farm. Moses Lefthand was with him. That's Lazarus' father. Moses is Blackfoot but he doesn't live on a reserve. He quit being an Indian and he took out his citizenship papers so he could vote and go in the beer parlour if he felt like it. He can read and write like a white man.

First thing he said, he asked me how Lazarus was doing in school and I said fine.

"First day he didn't do good." Moses doesn't wear braids; his hair is cut short so it's kind of spiky.

"First day none of the Grade Ones do so good, Mr. Lefthand."

"Yeah," Moses said. "But they don't climb under the desk and stay there."

"Well – a lot of 'em bawl," I said. "Lazarus didn't bawl."

"Damn right he didn't," Moses said. I was wondering if all Indians are built long and lean like Moses. He has a real deep voice. It is so deep it kind of buzzes against your chest. "All these kids gonna be at the depot for the royal train?"

I said they were and Jake let go the pump handle. Jake is built kind of like an Indian too when you think of it. He says that's from back-breaking work all his life from the time he kicked off the dew till the bed springs twanged at night. "Sure gonna be some reception," he said. "Crocus folks ain't had a hell of a lot to do with royalty, but they're sure goin' after her in high gear."

Moses had hold of a twig and he was sort of drawing in the ground with the end of it. Without looking up he said a funny thing. He said, "My folks – they was kings."

"Well, now," Jake said.

"Chiefs – same thing. Signed the Blackfoot Crossin' Treaty. My uncle – him an' the Queen. She was Queen Victoria."

"That's nice," Jake said. "You oughta be down there when the royal train rolls through."

"They asked us. Reception committee. Wanted us to wear feathers – Mrs. Lefthand to carry Lazarus in a *yo-kay-bo*."

"Did they?"

"We ain't."

"Ain't what?" Jake said.

"We'll dress proper – like Canadian citizens. Kid's too big to go in a *yo-kay-bo* on his ma's back anyways. I'm not paintin' myself. I'm not a spectacle. We don't wear moccasins no more. So they better get some Indians for that kinda stuff. Beads. Feathers. Porcupine quills. Green paint. That kinda stuff."

"M-hhmmm," Jake said.

"The Lefthands are Canadian just like other people. One hundred per cent altogether Canadian. We quit. They better get real Indians."

When Moses had left and Jake was sitting on a stool stripping Mary, in the barn, I asked him whether he figured the Prince and Princess would be going C.P. or C.N. He said both.

"I wonder what their train will be like, Jake?"

"They ain't goin' day coach, Kid."

"Bring it over on the boat with 'em?"

"Oh no. Probably take the Superintendent the railroad's special coach – right now they probably got her in the shops – paintin' her purple . . ." He quit.

"What, Jake?"

Jake looked up at me with his head against Mary's flank. 'Royal colour. Purple. Superintendent the railroad – his coach'd already be purple likely. They'll line her with red velvet – gold-plate the hot- an' cold-water taps."

"Paint a coat of arms on the caboose."

"Yeah." The milk started singing in the pail again. 'They'll be eatin' oysters an' lobster an' Winnipeg goldeye. Her an' alla their ladies-in-waitin'."

"Gee, Jake – I can hardly wait!"

I guess everybody was excited. In town it was all folks talked about – in the post office waiting for their mail – over at Malleable Brown's – MacTaggart's Trading Company – Repeat Golightly's Barber Shop. When Jake and me dropped in at Repeat's and Jake was stretched out in the chair, Repeat said: "Talk – hearin' lots of talk about the royal visit." He left off stropping the razor. "Ought to do somethin' about those blackheads there, Jake."

"Blow dirt – just blow dirt, Repeat."

"Enlarges the pores. Raises aitch with the pores. Lot of talk about this visit." He kind of lowered his voice the way he does and leaned over Jake. "Some folks not showin' the proper spirit."

"No!" Jake started to sit up.

"Hold still there. Can't shave a movin' object." Repeat pushed him back. "Not our own, mind you – not Crocus folks. Foreign element. Conception. Conception district. Few been in the shop."

"But what did they . . ."

"Not making a single preparation. Wonderful thing – royalty. I say royalty's a wond – "

"Yeh."

"Generation to generation." Repeat pulled up the skin under Jake's ear. "Aristocracy."

"Uh-huh."

"Figurehead the shipa state. Empire. Shade to the left. I like to look at the Empire like a crown. Struck me that way, crown. An' Crocus has her place there. Every single part the Empire's a jool."

"Yeah."

"Saskatchewan's one the jools." Repeat wiped off a fluff of lather onto the paper on Jake's chest. "You could say she was one the jools."

"Gettin' her down real fine when you come to towns like Crocus an' Conception, aren't you, Repeat?"

"Facet. One the facets one the jools."

"Huh?"

"Way a jool is cut. Facets. Faces, thousands faces. Facets." Repeat pumped Jake up straight. "Crocus is one of the facets in one the jools – set in the crown the Empire. Fifty cents. That'll be fifty cents, Jake."

Jake and me dropped in at Malleable Brown's and the bellows going *hawgh – hawgh*. Malleable said he was all set for the royal visit. He said he thought it was real nice and gracious and charming of the royal couple to save their visit till after harvest was over. While we walked over to MacTaggart's Trading Company we passed the Credit Union hall and heard the Crocus Band practisin' "Rule Britannia" under Mr. Tucker. I said to Jake it sounded fine and he said it sounded more like guerrilla warfare. When we got into MacTaggart's store, Mayor MacTaggart said:

"Wheels are rollin'. Set the machin'ry in motion. I.O.D.E. has been alerted. Women's Auxiliaries all the churches. Rot'ry – Activarians – Junior C. of C. Real burden the reception's being carried by the Crocus Disaster and Emergency Relief Committee."

"Disaster an' . . ."

"Just the official title," Mr. MacTaggart explained to Jake. "Already set up. For the occasion we've changed the purpose. Hig Wheeler's group has switched from Shelter and First Aid to decoration. Erecting an arch over at the depot covered with wheat and oats and flax and barley bundles. Sign in coloured lights – not like some communities."

"You mean Conception," Jake said.

"Aren't lifting a finger. No civic pride. We live up to our responsibilities. Homer Toovey – MacDougall Implement – supplying DDT."

"What the aitch for!"

"Stockyards and loading platforms. C'rrals – swamping them out – spraying them so's there won't be flies ner smells."

"That's nice," Jake said.

"Got a couple mounties from Brokenshell," Mr. MacTaggart said, "that can ride. Dress uniform. United Church choir's rolling. Flags – bunting – "

"Looks like one the facets one the jools is gonna twinkle."

"Huh?"

"Manner of speakin', Mac. What time of day does this royal train roll through?"

"Thursday afternoon."

"Yeh – I know – what time?"

"Why – say – come to think of it – I'm in the dark about that, Jake. Jus' went along thinking of the regular trains – this one's special. We'll slip over to the depot. Way-freight Brown'll know."

Over at the depot when Mr. Brown came to the wicket, Mr. MacTaggart asked him what time the royal train was stopping in Crocus.

"They are flyin' high over the grey Atlantic," Mr. Brown started off the way he talks like those C.P.R. travel folders. "In a luxuriously appointed strato-cruiser – high above the storms an' tempests – "

"Yeh – I know," Mr. MacTaggart cut in, "but what we were interested in – "

"Down the broad St. Lawrence, past quaint habitant Quebec to the hist'ried city of Montreal – "

"Way-freight," Jake said.

"Through the garden the Dominion – Niagara peninsula – North shore mighty Superior where green-clad pines stand their sentinel watch."

"How – long – are – they – stopping – off – here?" Mr.

MacTaggart said each word clear and slow.

Way-freight Brown looked kind of startled. "They aren't."

"Whaaat!"

"Take the Saskatchewan prairies faster'n a greased gopher through a thirty-six-inch thrashin' machine. Eager to catch their first glimpse of the soft swellin' beauty the Alberta foothills."

"They aren't even stoppin'!"

"Regina – Moose. Jaw – not here," said Mr. Brown. "Orders."

"Then all this preparation, all this work – it's been useless."

Jake said, "Couldn't you – uh – drop a line to the Superintendent the railroad, Way-freight?"

"Jake," Mr. Brown sighed, "the Superintendent this railroad doesn't even know I'm breathing in Crocus. When they tell me that train's takin' on water down the line at Conception – "

"Whaaat!"

"Huh!"

"Seven minutes – at Conception – got to take on water."

"You'll have to get it changed," Mr. MacTaggart said.

"Mac – nothing's going to get changed. Nobody tampers with this railroad."

"But they could change – "

"If you're looking for your true royalty in North America," Mr. Brown said, "you look at the railroad. There is aristocracy. If you wanta see a royal edict." He waved a sheaf of paper at Jake and Mr. MacTaggart. "Just you take a look at a railway time schedule."

Mr. MacTaggart took it pretty hard. Me and Jake went right along with him whilst he called the town council together. He explained to them how the royal train wasn't even stopping at Crocus – how she was stopping seven

minutes to take on water at Conception that hadn't even
lifted a finger to a royal welcome. All aitch broke loose
and Mr. MacTaggart rapped the table with his gavel.
Mr. Tucker that leads the band said they'd have to bring
pressure to bear; he said it wasn't any use getting up a
petition – have to write our pressure groups. Malleable
Brown asked what were pressure groups.

"When you want something, Malleable," Mr. Mac-
Taggart said, "you work on pressure groups."

"How do you start it rollin' then?" Malleable asked.
"We got any pressure groups here in Crocus?"

Mr. MacTaggart said they weren't pressure groups
exactly but they'd do: Rotary, Activarians, South Crocus
Homemakers, I.O.D.E. Whole meeting kind of blew up with
councillors shouting where to send letters to – asking for
the royal train· to take on water at Crocus instead of
Conception: provincial and federal members – Minister
Education – Minister Agriculture – Minister Lands and
Mines.

"Don't stop at Ottawa!" Mr. Tucker yelled. "Send 'em
to England!"

"Wouldn't even hurt to send one to Prime Minister
England," Malleable shouted.

"Sure," Merton Abercrombie jumped up. "To the Queen
– let the I.O.D.E. do that one. Tell 'em to remind her about
that quilt!"

"What quilt?" said Malleable Brown.

Over Mr. MacTaggart's gavel banging, Mr. Abercrombie
shouted, "One she sold to the I.O.D.E.!"

"She didn't sell any quilt to the I.O.D.E."

"Sure she did!"

"It was a rug she hooked. Couple million dollars!"

"All right – remind her that rug when they write!"

When Jake and me were riding back to the farm, I
asked Jake if he thought she'd work or not. Jake said he

didn't know, but they'd sure have to pay attention to those letters to railroad officials, cabinet ministers, Prime Minister. Couldn't ignore the South Crocus Homemakers, Activarians, Young C.C.F. Club, Crocus Caledonian Society of Knock-Out Curlers. Jake he figured they might have a fifty-fifty chance.

But Mr. MacTaggart wasn't the only one having trouble. Out at Rabbit Hill School Mariel Abercrombie and Cora Swengel tied for being the kid that would hand the flowers to the Princess. Miss Henchbaw said all right then we'll have a vote to see who it'll be. Cora Swengel won. Mariel bust out crying. She said her mother wouldn't come across with the flowers. Miss Henchbaw said she thought she would and Mariel cried worse so Miss Henchbaw got mad and she said she didn't like Mariel's attitude and Mariel said she didn't care and she ran out into the cloakroom. I told Jake and Moses Lefthand about it when I got home.

"Don't matter aitch of a lot now," Jake said. "Don't even know if the train's stoppin'."

"Why didn't they pick my kid Lazarus?" Moses said.

"S'posed to be the one with the high av'rage," I told him. "Grade Ones weren't in on it."

"Why not?" Moses said.

"Too little."

"My kid ain't little. He could hand flowers to somebody. He could do it."

"I guess she figgered it should be a older kid, Moses," Jake said.

"My kid's a Canadian kid," Moses said kind of stubborn. "My kid's a good size for his age."

"For his age . . . yeah . . . but . . ."

"She think he's little?" Moses turned to me.

"Search me, Moses. She wants one of the older kids."

"What's the difference?" Jake said. "The whole thing's all tangled up in the britchin' now."

"All the same," Moses said stubborn, "I'm gonna see this teacher. I got to find out about them Grade Ones where Lazarus is." He hitched up his Boss Of the Range pants. "Just in case."

It was a week later and folks still didn't know whether the Princess would even stop at Crocus, that Moses came to Rabbit Hill School. It was after four and I was cleaning off the blackboards.

He walked right up to her desk. She said "Hello" and Moses said:

"He doin' what you say?"

"Oh – yes – Mr. Lefthand. Lazarus is doing very well."

"Like the other kids?"

"He was a little shy at first . . ."

"Now – about these flowers."

"Flowers? I don't . . ."

"These Princess flowers. What you gonna do for the Grade Ones without flowers?"

"Oh – that. We had a little misunderstanding and . . ."

"I'd like my kid to do this."

"Oh," Miss Henchbaw said. "Oh."

"You forgot all about the Grade Ones when you picked your kid," Moses said and he stared down at her. "And my kid."

"Well, no. We have to be fair about it. All the children would love to do it. Their parents would . . ."

"He ain't small."

"I beg your pardon."

"Six years old. He's the right size for that. You better use a Grade One kid. It would be nice if you used Lazarus."

"Oh." Miss Henchbaw cleared her throat. "We – we can't change our plans now, Mr. Lefthand. It wouldn't be – uh – fair. Just – we try to run the classrooms in a democratic way."

"You do this democratic?"

"I think I did."

"Those Grade Ones – did they vote?"

"Why – well – they're so small . . ."

"Miss Henchbaw – I'm sorry you forgot all about those little Grade Ones."

"I suppose I . . ."

"Poor little Grade One," Moses said.

"There are only four of them."

"You know what that is?" Moses leaned over her desk. "They got no rights, your little Grade Ones. Minors. Just little minor group in your school, huh?" Miss Henchbaw didn't say anything. "Poor little Grade Ones," Moses said sad. "Can't give flowers. Can't take a crack at it. Poor little minor Grade Ones group."

"There are no minority groups in my school, Mr. Lefthand!" She just cracked it out.

"Yes."

"I – may have seemed – to overlook – what would you suggest, Mr. Lefthand?"

"This way. Give 'em each a nickel. Then they flip this nickel. Odd Grade One he gives the flowers."

"And what about the twos and threes and fours and the rest of the school?"

"Oh – I didn't think of that."

"Then your oversight" – Miss Henchbaw got up – "is much worse than mine, isn't it?"

"Yeah," Moses said. "Yeah."

I didn't hear what else they said because Miss Henchbaw noticed me and she said I better be going home.

"Sure a mess," Jake said. "Wranglin' about who's gonna give her flowers when they don't even know she's gonna stop off long enough to take 'em."

"Wonder how the council made out with those letters, Jake?"

"We'll find out, Kid. Cream can's full. You an' me'll see

Mac when we go into town this afternoon."

Mr. MacTaggart didn't look so cheerful. "Just going over to Way-freight's now," he told us. "See if there's any developments."

Jake and me went with him. Way-freight Brown looked up when we came in. He had that green eyeshade on whilst he sat at the telegraph key.

"We just took a dangle over," Mr. MacTaggart said. "See if there was any – ."

Way-freight cleared his throat. He looked kind of dazed. "First time in forty-two years' experience with this railroad – gentlemen – seen everything."

"That royal train," Mr. MacTaggart began.

"Just before you stepped through that door." Mr. Brown kind of brushed at his forehead, like he had a cobweb tickling it or something. "Came through. Been a change."

"Yeah?"

"Yeah!"

"Orders – slight change in orders."

"Concernin' takin' on water at Conception," Mr. MacTaggart prodded him.

"The royal train," Way-freight's voice took a kind of a skip and a jump, "trailin' her snowy plume of steam an' smoke across the wavin' fields of golden grain – takes on her water – uh – at Crocus." He quit and you could hear the telegraph key going to beat anything. "For this she will require – not the usual seven minutes – but eleven."

Everything got rolling; the band started practising again in the Credit Union Hall; they finished up the arch at the depot. The day of the royal visit folks came streaming into town from all over Crocus district – from Brokenshell and Macoun and Ogema and Tiger Lily and Wrist Hills. We drove into town with Baldy and Queen and the democrat and the Lefthands rode with us. Folks came in their cars and wagons jamming the whole down town.

Mrs. Lefthand and Lazarus they just sat in the democrat not saying anything. "We got to get near the front," Moses said and he looked down at the newspaper-wrapped parcel Lazarus had on his knee.

"Sure," Jake said.

And he did. We were right down there next the platform. I could see Mayor MacTaggart's hand trembling so the paper speech in his hand was shaking as he walked up and down, his lips moving. Then somebody at the east end of the crowd let out a yell. We heard her whistle.

She wasn't purple like Jake said. She stood there hissing and tinging whilst she took on water. Mr. Tucker and the band started up "Rule Britannia". Then I noticed Lazarus Lefthand had taken the paper off his bundle.

They weren't big floppy asters or golden glow or dahlias that won in the flower show. They were buffalo beans he'd picked off of the prairie and Indian paintbrush and brown-eyed Susans. He had them tight in his fist. They were wild-flowers.

"All right," Moses said, real husky. "Me an' Miss Hench-baw flipped. She lost. You go up there and give her them, Lazarus. When Miss Henchbaw says. Just walk up and hand 'em. You're citizen too. Hers. One hundred per cent. You got kings in you." He sort of gave Lazarus a push. "If you got to do your nose," he warned him, "don't snuff it loud. Use the sleeve. When nobody's lookin'."

Little Lazarus, he didn't curtsey like Cora Swengel when she gave her flowers. When the Princess took Lazarus' she smiled at him. She smiled at him and smelled his flowers and she said something to the Prince beside her.

She didn't smell Cora's but she smelled Lazarus' bouquet. The wild ones.

13

The Golden Jubilee Citizen

ONE THING I noticed: it's after the ice has gone out of the curling rink and before they can get on the land for spring drilling – that's when folks seem to stir up stuff they let lie all summer and fall. Holgar Petersen remembers the fight he had with Pete Snelgrove over that hay deal back in Nineteen Fourteen. Repeat Golightly gets sore all over again the way Chez Sadie's put in that barber chair instead of just giving women permanents the way they're supposed to do. Jake starts licking old wounds too.

Jake helps Ma and me farm our farm down Gover'ment Road from Crocus. Some of the wounds give Jake the worst twinges are the ones he got off of Miss Henchbaw that teaches us kids out at Rabbit Hill. She is a stickler for the truth; like Jake says, she stickles worse than anybody in Crocus. When she isn't stickling she is running Crocus. She doesn't run Jake.

Miss Henchbaw is the one organized the Crocus Pre-

servation of Historical Shrines and Historical Landmarks
Society – her and Repeat Golightly. That put her in the
saddle you might say, so when we run up against Saskatchewan's Jubilee Year, she's all set to run that too.

Take the day last fall when Jake and me were in Repeat's
barber shop. I already had my hair cut and Jake was laying
back in the chair – Repeat's razor was snickering up and
down his strop, and I hadn't been listening too hard because I was trying to figure out the time from the clock. It
is very hard to figure out the time when you are looking at
the face of a clock and it is backwards in the mirror over
Repeat's instrument shelf. She was that warm fall we had
last year and Repeat's door was open and every once in a
while a sort of a breeze would lift up the tufts of hair
around the chair and breathe them along.

"She didn't invent the Golden Jubilee, Repeat." It came
out sort of muffled the way the towel was wrapped all
around Jake's face except for the tip of his nose.

"No one says she did – didn't say she did." Repeat left
off stropping and took Jake's nose between his thumb and
finger with the little one up like women do with their tea-
cup. "But without Miss Henchbaw – without her – there'd
be no Golden Jubilee Committee." Repeat wiped his razor
on the square paper on Jake's wishbone. "To her and her
alone goes the credit – most the credit – for the programme
to mark our province's fiftieth birthday."

Jake grunted. He can get a lot into a grunt.

"Still there, Jake. Can't shave a moving object. Old-
timers."

"What about 'em?"

"Her thought of the benches – old-timer benches to be set
up on the down-town streets – Golden Jubilee Benches.
Hers was the Golden Jubilee Mosquito Control Programme."

"Was it?"

"Certainly. Certainly was. Oratorical contest What My Province Means To Me. She was the one put the bug in the Activarians' ear – about the contest."

I knew all about that. She was cracking the whip over us kids in Oral English, getting us to do speeches on What My Province Means To Me.

"That woman," Repeat was saying to Jake, "that woman has a great sense of history. Great sense."

"No sense."

"How's that, Jake?"

"Nothin'!"

Repeat turned away from the instrument shelf, dabbed at Jake with that after-shave stuff. "I'm qualified, Jake."

"That's nice."

"Qualified to judge whether or not she has historical sense." Repeat pumped Jake straight up. "She has."

"Well, I don't know, Repeat – "

"I do." Repeat plugged in the clippers. "Most the reading I do is historical reading. You might say I revel in history." Repeat bent his knees the way he does, lowered his head, started his first swath through Jake's hair. "Fabulous new best seller set in the time of Louis Quinzy." He lowered his voice to a whisper. " 'In Felice Gagnon's lovely body flowed warm Basque blood – spiced with a fiery Castile strain – she charmed the crowned heads Europe – held kingdoms in her graceful hands . . .' "

"That's nice. Take some off the top, Repeat."

" '. . . but her spirit was completely pagan'." Repeat turned off the clippers – picked up his comb and scissors. "Learn quite a lesson from history. As the history is bent so the nation groweth."

"Uh-huh," Jake said.

"Like a fellow's childhood – same thing as a human's childhood – nation's history."

"I guess so," Jake said.

Repeat straightened up, took a couple snips at the air with his scissors; he blew on his comb. "Good childhood – good nation."

"Uh-huh," Jake said.

"Moral lesson."

"Uh-huh," Jake said.

"Crocus and Saskatchewan has – have had – a colourful past. Colourful."

"Thunderin' hooves the mighty fur traders – like of that," Jake said.

"Wild elements – bred in the blood and bone of Crocus citizenry. Blood and bone."

"Don't forget the top, Repeat." Jake squinted up to him. "Most the folks I know – early days – hail from Ontario. They come out for free land or a chance to start out a general store from scratch. They just got Ontario in their blood an' bone. Kind of thin on the wild elements you was . . ."

"Can't take it too literally, Jake," Repeat said. "We *all* got Ontario in our blood. Isn't much can be done about that."

"No," Jake said. "I guess not." He looked kind of thoughtful.

"Let us not underestimate Miss Henchbaw. Her part – major part in the coming Golden Jubilee Celebrations."

"I won't," Jake said.

Repeat dusted Jake off with that duster. He whipped the sheet from around his neck. Jake got up and reached in his pocket.

"Sheer genius," Repeat said. "Two and a quarter, Jake."

"Uh-huh," Jake said.

"Sheer stroke of sheer genius when she figured out her idea – Crocus Golden Jubilee Citizen. Thanks, Jake."

I knew all about that too. Repeat meant the essay contest where you had to tell who you thought was Crocus

District's Golden Jubilee Citizen, the one person Crocus couldn't have done without during the last fifty years. That was what I was working on.

It didn't go so good; I noticed it's not so easy to get your words to pull together in the harness the way you want them to. Besides – it isn't so easy to figure out a thing like that. First off I thought of Old Daddy Johnston that's a hundred and seven. Jake said:

"Not Daddy, Kid. Daddy's already famous in a way. Way I see it – when they tell you to pick your Golden Jubilee Citizen, I figger they mean somebody a person wouldn't think of offhand. Somebody that's bin goin' along, doin' his job so you – well – sort of like you was holdin' up a lantern an' there he is – Crocus Golden Jubilee Citizen. Bin there all the time – till your lantern shone on him an' showed what he was really like."

"Mmmmmh."

"Now – I like Wing. Sanitary Café. All the folks thinkin' of Merton Abercrombie, bank manager – MacTaggart, mayor Crocus. Me – I like Wing in the Sanitary Café."

"How come, Jake?"

"Well – all durin' them dirty Thirties when he fed the bindle stiffs an' the stew bums – the scen'ry hogs an' the gay cats an' the lump bums that swung down off of the freights behind Hig Wheeler's Lumber Yards. Wing never let one of 'em go away hungry. You take the hockey outfits – Peewees, Juniors, Intermediates – ain't a year Wing didn't put up the money for their uniforms. Then all them baskets fruit he sends to anybody sick in the hospital. Go a long ways, Kid – before you find a better Golden Jubilee Citizen than Wing."

"Uh-huh. What about Doctor Fotherin'ham?"

Jake pursed his mouth. "Yeah. But don't forget the lantern, Kid. Doc's Federal Member. Had the lantern light throwed on him ever since he went down to Ottawa." Jake shook his head. "I still like Wing."

You never catch Jake following other folks' tracks very far. If you tried a hundred years you would have an aitch of a time to replace Jake. It was Jake taught me to hold a twenty-two and touch off a gopher. He's made me all kinds of things, because he's kind to kids. I never known him to thin a kid's hide once. When I was very young he used to hide the Easter eggs in the strawstack for me. You take in the olden days:

"I never picked my friends outa race ner politics ner religion," Jake says. "I was fussy about Wilf – Sir Wilf – an' I drunk Catawba wine with Sir John A. After we settled a little misunderstandin' me an' Looie got along well too."

I know this about Jake. He's honest and he's straight through. He has worked hard all his life and like he says:

"Every day my life I twanged the bedsprings at sundown an' I kicked the dew off of the stubble with the rooster. I never had a holiday long as I can remember. Who the hell ever heard of a hired man takin' a holiday!"

Jake could have been a politician. Like he told me once:

"I could of bin in the Senate – walked in velvet up to the fetlocks – smoked House of Senate cigars an' spit into gold goboons like the rest of 'em down there. I ain't. I'm a hired man. Except for a couple times in the year when she gets piled to the barn windows – it's cleaner."

Other fellows just let their minds coast along – but with Jake the motor's always going.

I guess it was along about March this spring, after I been chewing away at that essay, it suddenly dawned on me who ought to be Crocus Golden Jubilee Citizen. Like Jake said, it was like I held up a lantern and there he was in the circle yellow light: the man that made Looie Riel say uncle three times – once in English, once in Cree and the third time in French; the man that built the country; the man that invented hay wire; far as I was concerned the man the country couldn't have got along without. Jake Trumper – the Golden Jubilee Citizen and our hired man.

That essay just rolled along like tumbleweed. I put down all about how Jake can tell the weather and witch water wells. I told how he could call mallards and geese, moose, deer and pigs. I wrote how he could play the mandolin and sing "My Wild Rose of the Prairies" so you had a lump in your throat – how he was the fastest runner in the whole Northwest in his stocking feet.

It took five pages to tell the way he saved Chief Weaseltail and his whole band South Blackfoots from starving to death. I had her crackling and the pages scorching with the awful prairie fire of Nineteen Ten when he lost his horse, Buttermilk. The time he killed the grizzly in the Kananaskis Lakes when his gun froze up and all he had in his hands was his bare axe and so he split his skull right down the centre – the bear's. Then I ripped those pages out of my scribbler, because Kananaskis Lakes are in Alberta and I figured Miss Henchbaw she'd say we had to stick to Saskatchewan's Golden Jubilee and not slop over into Alberta. They're having one too.

I filled a whole scribbler with Jake.

It took three arithmetic periods and two nights to copy her all out in another scribbler. I turned the first one in to Miss Henchbaw. I wrapped up the other one and mailed her to Mr. Lambert that's editor of the *Crocus Breeze*.

One thing about Miss Henchbaw – she rips right through your stuff when you hand it in to her. I put it on her desk recess Monday morning. When we filed in and sat at our desks after dinner, she already had the coal oil on her fire. She snapped Steve Kiziw's head off for sharpening his pencil in the middle of "Pippa Passes": LaPrelle Rasmussen had her hand up clear through "The Empires of the Fertile Crescent" without Miss Henchbaw seeing it. When we got to "Now the Day is Over", Miss Henchbaw said she wanted to see me for a minute after the bell.

My scribbler about Jake being Crocus Golden Jubilee

Citizen lay on her desk next to a saucer of crocuses.

"I've read this." Her mouth got thinner. "You've done a commendable amount of work on it." She shifted "Trails through the Garden of Numbers" a little to the south. "It's too bad your subject matter couldn't have been a little more worthy of your effort." I waited for her whilst she took a piece of green chalk in her fingers and kind of fiddled with it. "Truth," she said and her face was red all the way to her hair she wears piled up like one of those round loaves of bread.

"Truth," she said again, "is like a pure spring welling from the ground. It must not be adulterated or contaminated. Its sparkling clarity can be so easily dulled and muddied."

I was wondering when she was going to get to my essay.

"We must strive after truth in word and deed." She picked up my scribbler with one hand whilst the other sort of tapped the green chalk on her desk top.

"This is not truth!" The chalk snapped like an old chicken bone. I watched the pieces roll off of the desk and onto the floor.

When I looked up, she was shaking her head, determined. "Louis Riel did not have dangling from his vest chain a rabbit's-foot watch fob!"

"When Jake rassled him on Cut Knife . . ."

"Nor did General Middleton wear a bobcat fur vest throughout his Eighteen Eighty-five campaign."

"Jake saw it!"

"I doubt it very much."

I stared at her and she stared at me and I guess you could call it a tie. She cleared her throat, sort of exasperated.

"This year – especially this year – our anniversary year, we cannot stand for impertinence with our province's history. I certainly can't agree with your selection for the greatest Golden Jubilee honour our district has to bestow."

I can't ever remember when I talked back to my ma or a grown-up in my life, let alone Miss Henchbaw. Same time I can't remember getting mad as quick as I did then – sick mad! "I figure he's a good . . ."

"By my calculations your nomination for Crocus Golden Jubilee Citizen – had been barely born by the time Louis Riel was hanged. He could hardly be a dignified symbol for our fifty years of history! He could hardly . . ."

That was when it happened – just like that green chalk snapping in her fingers. "He sure as aitch could! Maybe he doesn't smoke House of Senate cigars an' eat Winnipeg goldeye three times a day an' – an' spit into gold goboons an' wipe his mush with a silk napkin – but he is the greatest livin' human bein' I ever knew in my whole life!" I guess I even pounded on her desk because I was staring at my fist and it was all stuck up with a wad of yellow plasterseen.

When she spoke it was real gentle. "Then your choice is as valid as mine would be." Her mouth wasn't thin any more. "But I can't turn this in for possible publication to Mr. Lambert in the *Crocus Breeze*. You will have full credit for your English assignment." She brushed some of the green chalk crumbs off the desk top. "There are other crystal springs," she said. "That's all," she said. "You can go," she said.

Jake had already milked Noreen and Mary and Naomi and moved on to Ruth when I told him.

"She just said my Golden Jubilee Citizen wasn't any good, Jake."

"Did she?" The milk went on saying *some-fun – some-fun* into the pail.

"Nobody can be right but her," I said.

"Uh-huh." Jake turned his head up at me. "Who'd you pick?"

"Well – I – right now – I didn't intend to let this person know I picked him."

"Oh." The milk quit *some-fun – some-fun* and started saying *fun-fun-fun* as Jake stripped Ruth. "I guess it won't make much difference if you tell me." He got up to move the pail and stool down to Eglantine. "I won't breathe a word."

"You," I said.

"Huh!"

"I filled a whole scribbler all about Chief Weasel-tail and his South Blackfoots and Sir Wilfrid Laurier and Sir John A. I really . . ."

"No!" Jake straightened up so quick he knocked the milk pail flying. "Kid! You didn't."

"Sure. Her saying all about being impertinent with our history!"

"Not alla that – that . . ." Jake looked like his teeth were hurting him. "Stuff!" He swallowed and he sort of leaned back against Eglantine. Then his face brightened up. He let his breath all go out of him. "But she said she was damned if she was gonna send it into Chet at the *Crocus Breeze*!"

"Yeah," I said, "I didn't tell her."

"Tell her what?"

"What I did."

"What did you do?"

"Made another scribbler full word for word and sent it into Mr. Lambert myself. I wasn't taking any chances."

Jake was leaning up against Eglantine again. He looked like he needed to. He kind of brushed at his face with his hand like he had spider web tickling across his forehead. "Now," he said, "that's nice, ain't it!" I've seen Jake look that way before.

The time our fifty-bushel crop got hailed one hundred per cent.

The *Crocus Breeze* eight-page Golden Jubilee Edition came out May 24, because the town council figured that was the day to announce Crocus' Golden Jubilee Citizen.

My essay wasn't in it.

Mr. Lambert had his own essay. It took the whole front page. He called it: HOLD YOUR LANTERN HIGH.

This is what it said:

"We are an agricultural province celebrating our Golden Jubilee Year. Our fortunes have been tied to the land and to the grain that land grows for us. Today we wish to salute the man who for fifty years has been a living symbol of our grain-growing province. We wish to hold a lantern high and reveal that man in its golden light."

I had about lifting the lantern in my essay.

"Let us salute today the man who has seeded other people's grain when the summer fallow steamed under the spring sun, who has driven other men's teams when the meadow lark sang from the fence post. He has run other men's threshing machines and other men's binders. He has stooked other men's bundles when the strawstacks smoked against the far horizon. He has milked other men's cows, stretched other men's fences, done other men's chores."

I had in about chores and harvest.

"His fortunes have been tied to the land as surely as those of his employer, and to the vagaries, cruelties and generosities of prairie nature. This man suffered during the blue snow of Nineteen Six and Seven; he thirsted and went without during the dry Thirties. Hail hurt him as did grasshoppers and cutworm and sawfly and low wheat prices. If he walked through a field last fall, his overall pants turned blood red with rust.

"We venture to say that the bulk of our farm owners and operators today started out at some time in the past fifty years as hired men. If not as hired men then as boys who looked to the status of hired man as one of dignity, a place in farm life to be attained, a time to be reached when they could measure themselves against the worth of a grown hired man, a time when they could stook just as many stooks in a day as the hired man – a time when they could match him bundle for bundle when the threshing machine exhaled its slant plume of chaff and straw.

"This man eats at the same table as his employer and his employer's family, enjoying a social equality unknown in other parts of the world and in some other parts of our own country. He is a hay-wire mechanic, veterinarian, stock man, who answers to the name of hardtail, sod-buster, stubble-jumper, hoozier, or john.

"His genesis roves the world. He comes from Ontario, Galicia, Poland, Bohemia, Ukraine; he comes from south of the border, from Ireland, Wales, Scotland, Denmark, Norway, Sweden, Holland, Belgium. He wears flat-soled boots, has chores in his blood, straw in his overall bib and binder twine in his heart.

"He is in the pool of our lantern light now. You know him. Crocus' Golden Jubilee Citizen, without whom there could have been no fifty years of history, no Province of Saskatchewan:

"His name is Jake Trumper."

On Wednesdays the *Crocus Breeze* building sort of shimmies between Barney's Vulcanizing and Chez Sadie's: that's because Mr. Lambert is printing his paper for Thursday. It wasn't shimmying the twenty-fourth of May, when Jake and me walked in; there wasn't a soul on Main Street, them all being out at the fair grounds for the harness races and the Golden Jubilee Celebrations.

Mr. Lambert was all **alone** at the back by that machine that flips the round plate up and back and over again while he shoves sheets underneath and they print: NO SHOOTING or NO TRESPASSING or JUST MARRIED. He didn't hear Jake and me come up, but he turned when Jake tapped him on the shoulder with the rolled-up Golden Jubilee Issue of the *Crocus Breeze*.

"Well, Chet," Jake said.

"Jake. Kid."

"I just come to tell you, you got the wrong man in your lantern light, Chet."

Mr. Lambert squeezed out a black snake of ink onto the roller. "I don't think so."

"Me either," I said.

"Anyways," Jake said, "I figgered it was polite to come in an' tell you – uh – thanks."

"Don't thank me, Jake." He looked across the machine at me. He smiled a little. "Him."

"Oh," Jake said.

"Partly," Jake said, "you polished her up."

"No, I didn't," Mr. Lambert laid a new sheet down careful and reached up his hand. "I had enough to do with the special issue as it was. *Crocus Breeze* had a guest editor for the Golden Jubilee Issue."

"He wrote it up then," Jake said. "I'd like to . . ."

"*She* wrote it," Mr. Lambert said, "with certain discreet deletions and additions to the original piece." He looked over at me again.

Jake looked startled. "She?"

"Miss Henchbaw."

Jake swallowed.

I swallowed.

Once before I saw Jake looking that way. It was the time he knocked down nine grey Canada honkers in Tinchers' smooth-on barley field and Axel Petersen walked in on him.

That was two years ago, the fall Jake had forgot to get his licence. Axel Petersen is game warden for Greater Crocus District.

ABOUT THE AUTHOR

W. O. MITCHELL is a novelist, a playwright, a writer of short stories and a raconteur extraordinaire. His play *Back to Beulah* is performed across the country and is soon to be a motion picture. His novels have continued to sell steadily for over thirty years, and are favorites for course adoption at all levels across the country.

CANADA'S
GREATEST STORYTELLER

FARLEY MOWAT
Chronicler of man against the elements

Bestselling author, Farley Mowat, portrays true-life adventure and
survival with unique passion. His courageous stories of remote
lands, people and animals have been read in over twenty lan-
guages in more than forty countries. And now, the most cherished
of his stories can all be read in paperback.

The Mark of Canadian Bestsellers

FM-4